*For their constant love and attention
I dedicate this book to my daughters
Katherine, Paula and Christine.*

MIXED BLOOD

Silent Secrets

By
Adolph S. Konieczny

Printed in Victoria, BC, Canada.

ISBN: 978-1-4269-2684-6 (soft)
ISBN: 978-1-4269-2685-3 (hard)

Library of Congress Control Number: 2010904053

*Our mission is to efficiently provide the world's finest, most comprehensive book publishing
service, enabling every author to experience success. To find out how to publish your
book, your way, and have it available worldwide, visit us online at www.trafford.com*

Trafford rev. 3/23/2010

 www.trafford.com

North America & international
toll-free: 1 888 232 4444 (USA & Canada)
phone: 250 383 6864 ♦ fax: 812 355 4082

Notice, if you are interested in reading this novel called Mixed Blood II Silent Secrets, I suggest that you read my 1st book, "Mixed Blood." This will give you an insight as to how these characters evolved.

Rea LeaBeau

It had been several months since Astin passed away. Claudette sold their villa on the French Riviera and was moving into her grandmother's home in Paris. The home was situated with a view of the Eiffel Tower and the Arc de Triomphe. The land surrounding the home had a small vegetable garden with several flower gardens bordering the walkway to the front porch. It was very picturesque, painted yellow with white trim. There were four bedrooms on the second level, and one bedroom on the first floor. The basement had been renovated with two bedrooms and two baths all done in pleasant surroundings. The lower level of the home was used during the hot summer days. LeaBeau was a very pleasant and giving grandmother to Claudette and to people close to her. She enjoyed giving presents to her maid, cook, and gardener.

Rea owned two leather manufacturing plants; one on the outskirts of Paris, the other Casablanca, Morocco. Nearing her eightieth birthday, she continued to work every day. In 1907 she had telephone service installed in the plant in Morocco. This eliminated her trips to Morocco every two weeks. She gave most of the responsibilities to her trusted accountant Marcel, who had worked for her previously in her Paris plant for the past fourteen years. Marcel was promoted to assistant manager of the Casablanca plant. After several months she received a telephone call from her other trusted manager, Mika, who informed her that Marcel had left the job without notice and they had no idea where Marcel was or what had happened to him. He also informed her that there had been several break-ins to the hide cleaning factory and hundreds of hides had been stolen. He was told by some of his workers that the hides had been sold to a competitor in the neighboring town. He asked her to be urgent in sending someone to correct this problem. Her first thought was, I will have Alex, my great-grandson help me.

Alex

Alex was in his final month of receiving his doctorate degree in foreign language studies. It had been a long two and a half years at Oxford University where Alex was learning five different languages. There were many times during his studies that he found the work confusing and exhausting. He was told by the Dean of Languages that his doctorate degree would be forthcoming; only a short thesis on each of the languages was required. Alex was finding this to be the easiest part of his final work. He sometimes wondered what use there would be in speaking and writing in German, Spanish, Polish, Russian and French. He was looking forward to spending time with his mother, Claudette, and great-grandmother, Rea, in Paris. There would be much to talk about such as, what his intentions would be and how he planned to use his acquired knowledge in the coming years. No doubt, Claudette and Rea will have some ideas on what he would do. He had never lived or remained overnight in Rea's home but he would be there for the Bastille holiday, which was full of parades, bands, fireworks and people enjoying wine from different wineries in the southern part of France. He was well aware that Rea was against his studies of language which she saw as a waste of money and time.

Alex had finished his oral language presentation three weeks earlier and was in the process of clearing things out of his small efficiency apartment when he received a package by messenger from Oxford University. The package contained his written language thesis he had submitted. He also received a letter from the Chancellor of Oxford University, requesting him to be at his office the following morning at ten o'clock for an informal meeting. Alex was very pleased with the news he had received and he continued to finish packing his luggage for his trip to Paris. The following morning, dressed in his finest suit, he waited patiently in the outer chamber until the secretary called his name and escorted him to the Chancellor's office. The Chancellor congratulated Alex on his completion of his extremely difficult language studies. He also pointed out that there were several positions open in the government sector, should he be interested. He then handed Alex his doctorate degree and said there would always be a position open for him at Oxford, should he, at some later date, be interested. Alex thanked him for his offer and replied that there were certain things he wanted to do first.

Paris

With luggage in hand, Alex boarded a train for Dover, whereupon he boarded a ship for a short trip across the English Channel to CALAIS, then by train to Paris where the Bastille holiday was in full swing. The five-mile ride through the crowded streets seemed to take forever. Arriving at Rea's home that evening, Alex found only the maid and cook, who were happy to see him. The cook made a small dinner for Alex, who had not eaten any food that day. They informed Alex, that Claudette and Rea had gone for a short walk and would be arriving soon.

A short time later, they walked in to the dining room and were surprised to see Alex sitting at the table. He rose from his chair and greeted Claudette and Rea with hugs and kisses. They all sat down at the dining room table while, during dinner, an array of questions were asked about what his plans were for the future? Was there presently, a woman in his life? Did he intend to travel? Was he interested in teaching at Oxford University? Had it been offered? What was he interested in doing with his life?

Alex shook his head and said, "A woman in my life? No. Travel, maybe to Germany, Russia, and Poland. Yes, I have been offered a teaching position at Oxford University. What my interests are in the future, I do not know. Only time alone will tell."

Claudette took Alex by the arm and said, "Come, let me show you the rest of the house and where you will live while you are here."

Rea's bedroom was located on the main floor and Claudette was sleeping in one of the newly remodeled basement bedrooms. She told Alex that the other bedroom would be ideal, since the summer weather continued to be very hot and humid. Alex agreed and took his luggage to that spare bedroom. Both rooms had French doors that opened up to lush fragrant flower gardens.

The next few days were filled with the holiday spirit, delicious food, aromatic wine and good conversation which led Rea to ask Alex if he would like to see the leather manufacturing company and products that were made there. Alex had no choice but to go along with Rea's request.

"We will have breakfast at seven with Claudette, before she leaves for work at eight." Rea said.

The following morning, Claudette took Alex on a tour of the leather manufacturing plant. Alex did not like the smell of the plant at all. They entered the plant manager's office where he was given a pair of rubber hip boots and told he must wear them while walking in parts of the mill that were wet. A worker then took Alex to where the hides were being taken from a railroad car and hooked on large spikes about seven feet above the floor. There were maggots feeding on the raw pieces of meat that were left on the hides. The hides in a railroad car were busy crawling with maggots so deep that you could hardly see the hides they were chewing on. Alex became very sick at what he had just seen and moments later his breakfast was lying on the ground. The worker asked Alex if he was all right.

"No, I am sick!" After seeing the rest of the process involved in preparing the hides for jackets and an assortment of other leather uses, Alex was convinced that he would never become or want to work in a company such as this. Back at the office, he removed his boots and said to Claudette, "I have just experienced one of the worst things I have ever seen and I am sure that this is one company I would not want to work for."

She replied, "I felt the same way when I saw all those hides full of maggots, however, you will get used to seeing that and in time it will not bother you at all. Rea would like to see you in her office and I do not know why."

Alex mumbled to himself, on the way to Rea's office, that he had to find a way to politely refuse a job at this company. Rea saw Alex approaching her office and opened the door for him.

"Well, did you enjoy your visit throughout the plant?"

"Truthfully, I got quite sick when I was watching the men unloading animal hides from the railroad car. I had never seen anything like that before and it sickened me to the point of vomiting my breakfast."

Rea said that was understandable.

"I think we should have warned you what to expect. I want you to listen to what I am about to tell you. Please listen carefully. Our accountant, Marcel, at our leather company in Casablanca left without notice. No one has any idea where he might be at the present time. I was also informed by my plant manager that over a thousand cleaned animal hides were stolen from the storage building. Mika expressed concern over what our workers were told by some of their friends who are employees of the Luster Company. They had overheard reports that the Luster Company had just purchased a large quantity of prepared hides."

"Sounds suspicious," commented Alex.

Rea nodded and went on, "With that many hides gone, we had to shut down most of our operation for two weeks. I am asking you to go down to my company in Casablanca and speak with the plant manager about all of the information he and the workers can give you concerning this matter. Will you please do this for me?"

There was no way of saying no to the look that Rea was giving Alex.

Rea continued, "There is also a French Foreign Legion garrison on the outskirts of the city. I have known the company commander for several years and he will assist you in your search. His name is Dan Dupree. I will give you a letter of introduction that you can give him when you meet.

Alex told Rea that he was uncomfortable with this situation and felt like he was in a dark room with no windows or doors. He told Rea that he would try to do the best he could with no promise as to whether or not he could solve this problem. Rea gave Alex an envelope marked Commander Dan Dupree plus tickets for travel from Paris to Casablanca.

"Your trip will start by train to a small town of Cadiz located in Spain, near the rock of Gibraltar. Then you will travel by ferry boat to Tangier, then by rail to your final destination, Casablanca. In Casablanca a porter will take your luggage to a local carriage where you will inform the driver that you wish to go to a hotel called the Café Gray Hotel. Hand this letter of introduction to the desk clerk who will have a porter take your luggage to my apartment of three rooms. One is a small kitchenette, fully stocked with canned food or you can order any food by ringing the clerk any time of the day or night. There is a small sitting room and next to that room is a full bedroom with shower and bath facilities. I suggest you turn on the swamp cooler which not only cools the apartment but also allows moist air into the apartment. The air is very dry and hot at this time of the year. It is not necessary to compensate any of the people that perform any service for you as they are paid well by the accountant at the company office. He can be relied on as he was previously an assistant to the accountant Marcel that left the company several weeks ago."

Alex asked, Rea. "When should I leave for Morocco?"

Rea replied, "The sooner the better. Why not leave the day after tomorrow, which is Wednesday."

Leaving her office, Alex found Claudette and explained the discussion he had with Rea.

Claudette told Alex, "Rea has to have someone she could trust to solve the problems in Morocco."

Alex looked at Claudette, and said, "I have only been here four days and now I am leaving to face the obstacles and problems in Casablanca."

"You will do just fine. You are a smart young man and I am sure you will whip this problem in a very short time and come back to Paris." She gave Alex a warm motherly hug and said, "I love you very much and please call me any time."

"I will call you during office hours."

"Remember to call if you have some good news for Rea and me."

Alex arrived at Rea's home in mid-afternoon. He took his three pieces of luggage from the closet. The smallest one had all the papers from his language studies and his doctorate degree in language which was neatly covered with a glass frame. He decided to leave that piece of luggage in the closet. The other two pieces of luggage would travel with him to Morocco.

Tuesday evening, the cook had prepared a farewell dinner for Alex with fresh pork ribs, several entrées and a delicious red wine, of which Alex consumed several glasses in a short period of time.

Claudette came over to Alex and said, "Come with me. I will take you to your bedroom so you can get some sleep. Your train leaves at seven and you need to be up by five."

Holding tightly onto Claudette's arm Alex murmured in a very low voice, "I think I had too much wine and right now I need my bed. Thank you for taking me there."

The following morning, still fully dressed, except for his shoes lying next to his bed, Alex was awakened by the loud bell of the alarm clock. In the bathroom, he took a quick shower as cold as he could stand it. Then, he brushed his teeth, dressed, and with his hair combed, took his two pieces of luggage to the entryway. The cook was making poached eggs with bacon, coffee and bread. Alex sat down at the kitchen table and started to eat. Rea and Claudette came in and sat next to him.

They both smiled and Rea said, "Did you have a good time last evening?"

Alex replied, "Yes, but only just the time I can remember. I sort of lost my way after the third glass of wine." They finished breakfast and said their goodbyes as he entered the waiting taxi.

Sylvia

Arriving at the train station, he gave his luggage to a porter whom he followed to his compartment on the train. As the train was leaving the station the conductor came in with a young lady standing behind him, asking Alex if he could see his boarding ticket. Alex presented his ticket and after a short period of time the conductor turned to the young woman and said, "This gentleman has the same ticket number that you have. His was purchased five days ago, and yours was purchased today. So, I know it is he who has the right to this compartment. I am sorry, Madame."

Alex rose from his seat, looked at the conductor and said, "There is plenty of room in this compartment. I do not mind sharing it."

"I thank you for sharing. My name is Sylvia Mundi and you, sir?"

With extended hands they shook.

Alex introduced himself by saying, "I am Alex VanEpp, pleased to meet you. Please be seated down as the train is leaving the station for Gibraltar."

During the trip, Sylvia asked Alex, where he was going. Alex told her he was going to Casablanca to do some work for his great-grandmother at her leather company. He also told her that he had just graduated with a doctorate degree in foreign language and it would be a good time to use some of that knowledge while he was there.

He then asked Sylvia, "What brings you on this journey to Casablanca?"

Sylvia said she was being sent by her superiors of the high courts, on an investigation dealing with important priorities and conflicts of interest by certain individuals. "Yes, I am a trained judge and investigator."

Alex said, "I might need someone with your type of ability to settle problems that I might encounter."

They arrived at the port city of Cadiz and had a porter put their luggage on the ferryboat that would take them to Tangier, Morocco. It was a three-hour ride and they both decided to have lunch at the restaurant on the boat. The food was very good but the wine had a flat bitter taste. Alex looked over at Sylvia, who was finishing her second glass of wine, and could see that she was enjoying her glasses of wine, talking and laughing, between sips. Alex and Sylvia relaxed in the lounge chairs where she immediately fell asleep. Two hours later, as they were arriving at the dock in Tangier, Alex nudged Sylvia that it was time to wake up. Her first response was that she had consumed too much wine, and now had a headache.

"I have aspirins in my pocketbook, Alex, would you please get me some water?" which Alex did.

Sitting on the edge of the lounge chair, she took the aspirin with the glass of water. The porter took their luggage to the train leaving for Casablanca. Sylvia apologized to Alex for not being good company on the ferryboat. He said no apology was necessary. They both needed time to relax.

Alex turned to Sylvia and said, "Do you have a place to stay when we arrive?"

"Yes I am staying at the Café Gray Hotel."

Alex smiled and said, "This could only happen once in a lifetime. I have my great-grandmother's efficiency apartment in the same hotel."

They both had a good laugh about the coincidence in their lives. "Maybe some good things will happen," Sylvia replied, with a smile on her face.

Casablanca

Apparently, someone had notified the hotel of his arrival and the porter with the carriage asked if he was Mr. VanEpp, to which he replied, Yes.".

With their luggage they boarded a very cramped carriage, and after the two-mile journey, they arrived at Café Gray Hotel. Alex gave the manager a letter of introduction from Rea. Sylvia presented her credentials and was given a room across the hall from Alex's apartment.

"Sylvia, would you like to join me for dinner?

She replied, "Yes, I would. What time is good for you?"

The manager replied, "Dinner is at eight."

He turned to the manager and said, "Will dinner at seven be a problem?"

"No problem at all," replied the manager.

Alex turned to Sylvia, "Let's make it seven, then. That gives us time to freshen up."

Shortly before seven Alex arrived at Sylvia's door, knocked gently and said, "I am ready if you are."

She opened the door and wearing a low-cut blue dress said "Let's eat."

The dining room was quite warm and the bamboo fans did little to cool it. They ordered a beef stuffed roll with a lemon-lime sauce, potato, salad and a bottle of Bordeaux red wine. Dinner was complete with a raspberry cream sauce on a delicate white cake. Alex looked at his watch, it was already nine.

He turned to Sylvia and said, "I have got to get some sleep. Tomorrow is going to be a very busy day. I will walk you to your room."

She thanked him for the dinner, gave him a long, sensuous kiss, said goodnight and went into her room. Alex went into the apartment, where it was hot and humid. He immediately turned on the swamp cooler, which slowly cooled the room down to a very comfortable temperature. He undressed and just wearing his pajama pants he fell asleep immediately. Shortly, Alex was awakened by a knocking on his door. He rose from bed, opened the door and saw Sylvia standing there.

"What is wrong?"

"It is so hot in my room that I cannot sleep. Do you have any extra fans in your room?"

"No, but come in."

"Oh, it is so cool in your room. Please let me sleep on your couch. I will lock my door and be right back."

Before Alex could reply, Sylvia had locked her door and was back in his apartment with a light blanket and pillow.

Alex said, "You do not have to sleep on that couch, the bed is large enough for both of us. You can sleep on top of the bed sheets with your pillow, and I will sleep under the sheets, on one side of the bed, if that is all right with you?"

They both fell asleep in their respective places until the alarm clock rang loudly. Alex looked at the time and it was six am. He turned toward Sylvia and for the first time noticed how pretty she was sleeping there in the morning light.

Alex softly spoke to Sylvia and said, "It is time to wake-up, Sylvia."

Alex quickly showered, dressed, had breakfast and then left for his great-grandmother's leather company.

The Search

The ride through the crowded streets took a long time but finally he arrived at the LeaBeau Leather Company. Stopping at the entrance the manager stepped forward and asked politely,

"Are you Alex VanEpp?"

"Yes, I am and you are?"

"My name is Mika Bilton."

They walked together into his office whereupon Alex said, "I would like you to give me all the information you can leading up to the present time, regarding the loss of the animal hides from your storeroom. Also, we need someone to document what is being said, as a reference for me, in this investigation."

Mika stepped out of the office and soon returned with an elderly woman who could take dictation in French so their conversation could be reviewed at a later time.

Alex asked Mika, "Are you sure that this woman can be trusted to keep this confidential?"

Mika replied with a smile, "She is my mother-in-law."

Mika started the conversation. "Three weeks ago we received two railroad cars of hides from our supplier in Africa. Most of the hides were in very good condition. Due to the month long journey the maggots ate most of the fat and meat from the hides. The hides were hung in our warehouse and the final count was one thousand, one hundred and twenty. Of that number, thirty-one hides were so badly decomposed that they had no value at all and were placed in a small cement building where maggots could feed on them. These maggots are the primary source of cleaning hides. The final thousand and eighty-nine hides left were placed on the hanging racks in the storage building. It was locked on Friday night.

The following Monday morning my foreman came to me and said there are only a few hides left in the storage building. The rest were all gone. I went to look for myself and yes, the storage building was empty. I called all the workers together and told them that since we did not have any hides, there was no work to be done. There were hides coming from Russia, but when they would arrive was uncertain. I sent them home.

Two carloads of hides arrived yesterday and preparation of the hides has begun. I also received a report from my foreman, who was told by two of his workers that they overheard a worker say that he was the one who unlocked the door to the hide storage building. The worker was planning to leave his job after he received his money from the manager of the Luster Leather Company and after the wagons came in and loaded all of the prepared hides. The hides were to be taken to a storage building next to the Luster Company."

The foreman came into the office with the suspected worker. Mika asked the worker if he was the one who unlocked the hides' storage building. The worker, who seemed to be in a poor state of mind answered immediately, that yes, he was the one that opened the storage building on a Saturday evening to allow the wagons from the Luster Company to take the hides. He also said that the Luster Company was going to pay him a large amount of money for helping them. Mika asked the worker, "Who did you talk to at the Luster Company about arranging this robbery"

"It was the owner, Mr. Visser, a German."

Mika told the worker that he should not talk to anyone about the robbery and also told the foreman that he must stay in close contact with this worker and not allow him to speak to anyone until this robbery is solved."

Mika took a drink of tea. "Alex, Casablanca has a very small police force, poorly trained and not aggressive in solving any killings or robberies in the city. Be very careful of where you go and be sure that you are back at your hotel by seven in the evening. This whole area is instead patrolled by soldiers of the French Foreign Legion. They would be the ones to contact if you need any information about the theft of the animal skins from our building."

14

It was noon. Alex thanked Mika for all the information he had received and with the notes of their conversation, he left. Alex returned to the hotel for a small lunch and told the clerk that he would like to have dinner at seven that evening. He then stepped out to the road and asked the first carriage driver if he knew where the French Foreign Legion compound was?

The carriage driver replied, "Yes and I also know the commander, Dan Dupree." Finally, after a ten mile ride out to a desolate area they reached the Foreign Legion's garrison.

"There are two hundred and forty men stationed here, most of them sentenced here for crimes in France," said the carriage driver. "Should I wait for you?"

"No," replied, Alex, "But do come back for me at four and wait for me even if I am not at the gate. Be sure that you wait for me," he repeated.

The driver nodded his head in agreement and drove off.

The soldier at the gate came forward and asked Alex, "What is your business here?!"

"I have a letter for your commander, Dan Dupree," stated Alex.

The soldier said, "I must search for any weapons you might be carrying. If you have any weapons please give them to me now."

"I have no weapons," Alex replied.

The guard said, "Stand with arms outstretched while I search you."

With the search completed, Alex was taken to the headquarters of Dan Dupree. He introduced himself, stating that he was the great-grandson of Rea LeaBeau and handed him Rea's letter.

After reading the letter, Commander Dupree asked Alex, "What can I help you with?"

"I am searching for information about hides that were stolen from the LeaBeau Leather Company. I am hopeful I can recover and return them back to the company. Can you help me with this problem?"

Dupree responded by saying that except for a few enlisted men, the rest were killers and thieves who had the option to either go to prison or become soldiers for fifteen years in the French Foreign Legion. "It is not a very honest group of men but they know that if they try to desert, they will be found and shot. Since I have been in command for the last fourteen years there have been no killings or thefts by these men. I trust them and they trust me. Tomorrow we will try to find out who committed this robbery."

Alex left and when he reached the gate he found the carriage driver waiting as he had requested. As they were leaving the garrison, Alex told the driver to take him to the Café Gray Hotel, as it was after five and he was done for the day. When they arrived, he told the driverto be at the hotel promptly at nine on the following morning. The driver nodded his head in agreement and asked for money for his services on this day.

Alex told the driver "I will pay you tomorrow." The driver was motioning his hands that he wanted to be paid now!

Alex replied with a shout, "Tomorrow!" Then he went directly to his room, set his alarm to wake him in one hour and fell asleep at once.

Surprise

Alex awoke around six, took a quick shower, dressed in clean clothing and went to the dining room. While looking over the menu, Sylvia approached Alex and asked, "Would you like some company?"

"Sure", Alex replied. "It is always nice to have company with someone like you."

She smiled, "That is the most flattering remark, you have made since we left Paris."

"I will try to be more flattering in the future."

They ordered dinner and a bottle of Burgundy wine. With dinner finished, they took what was left in the bottle to a table in the bar where they had the waiter bring them glasses.

Sipping his wine, Alex asked Sylvia, "Did you have a good day with people in the courts?"

"It is difficult to get answers from people who are involved in some form of corruption. I will keep searching until I get some meaningful answers. And you, Alex, what have you accomplished?"

"Not very much, I have spent most of the time just finding out what happened and who could be of help."

Alex had the waiter bring another bottle of Burgundy wine and as they continued to drink, Sylvia said she had heard about the robbery at the leather company and that the commander of the French Foreign Legion was now in charge of solving the robbery.

Alex said, "I have already talked with him and he said he was going to help. I will see what develops in the coming days." Alex looked at his watch and said, "It is nine-thirty and I have got to get some sleep."

Sylvia said, "You cannot go to sleep. We still have a considerable amount of wine left. We can take it to your room for a nighttime drink."

"That is fine, bring it along."

Together, with unsteady steps, they arrived at Alex's apartment, which was cool and comfortable. Alex was lying in his bed and had not noticed that Sylvia had removed all of her clothing except her undergarments. She began to help Alex remove his clothing while she was kissing and touching his sensitive parts. They made passionate love for the next two hours. Then Sylvia reached over to the table, poured a glass of wine that they both shared. They continued to arouse each other until, during a moment of rest, sleep overcame both of them.

The alarm went off at its usual time of six. Sylvia rolled over on top of Alex and said, "More?"

Alex responded, "Yes." and continued with untiring love for the next hour.

They showered together and Sylvia, told Alex. "You are a fantastic lover!"

He replied, "The last time I made love to anyone was seven years ago when I was a senior studying at Oxford University. That is a long story and it is not worth telling."

They both dressed and went to the dining room for breakfast. It was already past nine. After they ordered breakfast Alex told Sylvia that he had to tell the taxi driver to wait, which he did and returned moments later.

LeaBeau Company

Sylvia asked Alex if she could ride in his taxi. Together they rode to the court house. As Sylvia was leaving, she turned, looked at Alex and said "Will I see you for dinner tonight?"

"Yes," Alex replied.

He then instructed the driver take him to the leather factory and once again, the driver demanded payment for his services. Alex decided it was time to pay his driver, which he did and also included a sizable tip which brought an ear-to-ear smile on his face. Alex questioned the manager if there were any new developments regarding the robbery or were there any markings on the hides that would confirm that they were the property of the LeaBeau Company?

"Just one moment," The manager left the office and returned shortly with an elderly man who said he was the hide selector.

"It was my job to mark the hides and indicated with my mark, which hides were selected for jackets, coats, boots, and several other items."

"Could you identify where the mark on each hide was located?"

"A blue mark always appeared on the front left side of the hide. Also, a corresponding number appeared in Roman numerals in the same area."

Alex confused, questioned the manager by asking him how he was able to keep track of 1000 hides by using just 10 Roman numerals?

The manager replied, "I will give you an example; Let us take the number five. That number may be used over and over again and in some cases the hides marked with that number could be any amount within the given number of hides. Only that number is used in making a particular product, such as finished leather for coats. Other numbers are used for several other items that we process here."

Alex left for the garrison to talk with Dan Dupree and told Dupree of his meeting with the company manager and the system they used for marking the hides. Dupree found that information to be very interesting and important in the investigation.

"Now I need to have a meeting with the one person that was involved in the robbery of the hides" Dupree told Alex. "Let us meet at ten tomorrow with your company manager tomorrow and the person involved."

Alex had the taxi take him back to the company office where Alex told the manager of his meeting with Dupree and that the man involved should be at his office tomorrow morning at ten.

It was five in the afternoon when Alex arrived back at the hotel. He told the desk clerk to reserve a table for dinner at seven. He then went to his room and tired and dusty took a shower, dressed and slumped into a well cushioned chair for a short nap. The aroma of Sylvia's perfume still lingered, as he fell asleep. A knock on the door startled Alex from his sleep, "Who is there?"

A voice replied, "I am the desk clerk. It is seven. Are you planning to have dinner?

Alex replied "Yes, I will be right there. Thank you for waking me."

For dinner, he ordered fried fish, salad with rice and a glass of Chablis wine. Midway through his dinner Sylvia arrived and said she was sorry for being late, sat down and removed a portion of Alex's dinner onto her plate. Then she filled her wine glass, and while doing so asked Alex, "What kind of a day did you have?"

He replied. "I was busy gathering information about the robbery.

What was your day like Sylvia?"

"No one wants to get involved and those that do seem to tell me nothing but lies. No one wants to tell me the truth. They have a brotherhood that protects each of them. I think tomorrow I will take off my wedding ring and act more like a single woman with a very sexy approach to my questions."

Alex was surprised, "Sylvia. I did not realize that you were married."

She said, "I have been married for three years to a very smart man who is a diplomat in foreign affairs. He is a mullato whose father is from somewhere in Africa. His mother who is white and French is a professor in a small university near Paris. What about your parents?"

"My mother is the grand-daughter of Rea LeaBeau who owns this leather company in Casablanca and another on the outskirts of Paris. I do not know too much about my father. From what my mother told me, my paternal grandmother was born in Georgia, a state in America. My father is white and so is my mother.

With dinner finished and each wine glass empty, they retired to their respective rooms. Upon entering his room, Alex noticed a bottle of wine covered in ice with a note from Sylvia, saying, "If you want to talk and have a cold glass of wine, tap twice, on my door."

Alex tapped twice on her door and Sylvia softly responded, "One moment. Alex, go wait in your room, I will be there shortly."

As Alex was opening the bottle of wine, Sylvia entered in a stunning négligée.

Alex said "That négligée that you are wearing would capture the attention of anyone that had the pleasure of seeing you wearing it. You look beautiful and sexy. Yes, very sexy."

Sylvia replied that she purchased it for an unusually low price, from a vendor who said he lived in Libya and it was once worn by a family princess.

As the evening wore on, they continued to talk. As Alex poured the last glasses of wine, Sylvia stepped out of her négligée and kissing Alex said, "Come to bed with me."

Together, into the late evening, they made passionate love with Sylvia pressing Alex to perform more and more until he was exhausted. He fell asleep in her embrace, silently sleeping until he was awakened by the alarm clock. Still lying in bed, he started to remember, what a beautiful evening and night he had with Sylvia. Was he falling in love? Maybe.

Bad News

After a quick shower and breakfast, Alex found his driver waiting for his arrival and told him that he had to return to the office of the leather company. Arriving at the office just before ten, Alex saw Commander Dan Dupree, the manager and his trusted foreman in the office. He walked in, greeted everyone and said, "I hope you have some good news today."

The manager said, "We have some bad news! My foreman tells me that some time during last night or early this morning, the witness, somehow unlocked the doors that kept him from coming out of the room where he was being held. We had no idea where he might be until Cmdr. Dupree arrived. Dupree said that two of his men doing night patrol in the slum district may have found something and suggested that we look at the person in the wagon and verify if he was our witness. The foreman and I looked at the dead person. He was found in the slum part of the city at the end of a cluttered alley. He had been stabbed several times, and his throat had been slashed. The only thing found on the body was a piece of hide in his hand that bore the letter V in purple. The foreman and I looked at the dead person and agreed that it was our witness."

The elderly man who was the Collector came into the office and looked at the V marking on the piece of hide and said, "Yes that is my mark. The V is for the Roman numeral five."

Cmdr. Dupree told the manager, "Mika that V although it was not much evidence, was still enough to make a search of the Luster Company owned by a German named Visser."

Alex asked Dupree if he could accompany him on the search of the Luster mill property.

Dupree agreed and said, "We will have to go to the garrison where I will pick out 25 men to help search for evidence of stolen hides."

It was late afternoon when they arrived at the Luster Leather Company. Visser met Dupree at the entrance to the building. "What brings you here, Commander?"

"We are investigating the theft of animal hides from the Rea LeaBeau Leather Company. Will you give us permission to search your property?"

"Oh no, you cannot do that. We have many new tanning processes that we do not want to share with anyone else." He looked at Alex and said, "Who is this man, Commander?"

"He is the great-grandson of Rea LeaBeau and is acting in her place."

"That fact is more the reason why I would not allow him to go through my company."

Dan Dupree turned to Alex and said "Stay here with one of my men and the rest of us will search this property."

Visser shouting at Dupree, and yelled, "You cannot come in here! I will call the police, if you so much as try to enter any of my building."

Dupree replied, "WE are the police and WE will inspect your building! Now unlock this door into the building!"

As the door swung open, it exposed a room full of hides hanging from racks. Alex and Dupree, inspecting the hides noticed there were purple markers found on every hide that they inspected. Each were Roman numeral five marks. After looking at a considerable amount of hides and finding the same purple marks on all of them, he went to the door where Visser was standing and said, "Do you have a type of mark on your hides?"

"No. There is no type of mark that is put on any of my hides. We never do that."

Dupree had him look at some of the hides, which had the marks from the LeaBeau Leather Company. Visser tried to cover his remarks by saying, "Those marks must have been made by the shipper of the hides and I had forgotten that they had been marked."

"That is a feeble statement with no merit whatsoever,"

Visser was placed under arrest, along with six of his workers and put in the local jail to await trial in the following week. Commander Dupree ordered that all the hides at the Luster Company should be moved to the LeaBeau Company immediately.

Days before the trial, Visser complained of stomach problems by the bad food that they were given and the stench from the sink and toilet in their cell. Visser was allowed out of his cell to use the toilet facilities outside the building, but not returning with his guard, two soldiers went to investigate. They found the guard badly beaten and near death. Also his revolver and a strap of bullets were gone. The search for Visser continued, with no success. They only had one clue. He withdrew all of his money from the bank and no one had any knowledge of where he had gone.

Victory

Sylvia was replacing the one judges of the trial who had been ill for several days. Commander Dan Dupree presented all the necessary information about the Luster Company and the death of one of his soldiers by Visser, whose whereabouts, at this time, was not known. After hearing all the evidence, Sylvia and two remaining Judges left for their chambers to discuss a final decision on this case. Returning, the eldest judge read the decision which awarded LeaBeau Leather Company full compensation and acquisition of the Luster Company, for the amount of four hundred thousand francs, if that was agreeable with Alex VanEpp.

His reply was "Yes. Of that amount, Commander Dan Dupree will receive forty thousand francs."

Alex thanked the courts, left immediately for his bank and withdrew the money for the Luster Company and Dupree's services. Then he hurried to the company office where he told Mika what happened. Now that the Luster Company was also owned by the LeaBeau Leather Company, Alex would in charge of both companies for making important business decisions. Some of those decisions included deciding what men would be promoted to be in charge of each of the companies and deciding to double Mika's salary.

Triumph

Alex returned to the hotel extremely pleased with what he had accomplished that day. He had not realized the time was already six and checking the front desk, he told the clerk that he would like his dinner at seven. Entering his room, he saw Sylvia, who yelled "Congratulations on your acquisition of the Luster Company. You will soon become a millionaire."

They both hugged and kissed while they laughed together. At the dinner table, Alex turned to Sylvia and said, "You were a great help today. How will I ever be able to repay you?"

Sylvia replied slyly, "Tonight, Alex, tonight."

Dinner was delicious, sea trout cooked in palm oil with a dash of lemon and mint, surrounded by oysters and white Bella wine from Italy complemented the meal.

In Alex's apartment, he opened a bottle of wine and a note from the hotel manager saying "Congratulations and compliments to you, sir. signed, Café Gray Hotel."

While drinking their glasses of, Alex told Sylvia that he would be leaving tomorrow for Paris. He forgot to mention that he had talked with his mother, Claudette, and told her briefly what had happened. When he arrived home, he would give them a full accounting of what had transpired in the past months.

He and Sylvia make passionate love through the evening and into the following morning.

Sylvia told Alex, "I am going to miss you and I have enjoyed the pleasures of your love, time and time again. I hope to see you when I return to Paris next month."

Alex, speaking in a soft voice, said "I will miss you for your love and affection that made me feel like a man again. Your image has captured my heart and mind and I find it difficult to let you go."

The Journey

When Alex awoke at eight thirty, there was a note lying next to the alarm clock. It simply said, "I love you, Sylvia." He washed, packed his luggage and then went to have breakfast. He found the manager at the clerk's desk and asked him if there were any ships traveling from Casablanca to the coast of France?

He replied, "There is a Portuguese freighter that leaves for Le Havre, France at eight this evening. It is a four day trip and I have taken that trip with my family many times. The rooms are comfortable and clean and the food is fair."

Alex thanked him for the information, and the courtesy given during his stay at the hotel. The porter left his luggage stacked at the entrance of the hotel. It was now eleven. He told the driver to stop at the LeaBeau factory. He wanted to give Mika a letter of authority for control of the operations of both companies. He also handed the accountant a note, signed by Alex, that Mika's salary would be doubled. Mika thanked Alex for this opportunity and told him that he would do everything in his power to improve the welfare of the workers and the profit of the companies.

Alex had the driver stop at the courthouse, in hopes of saying goodbye to Sylvia and asked about her whereabouts. He was informed that she was investigating some problems at a court some fifty miles east of here and would not be available the rest of the day. He then directed his driver to take him to the Portuguese ship, which would be leaving the dock at seven this evening. He checked with the dock purser to see if they had any cabins available. He replied that one cabin had been made available early that afternoon, by a Mr. Visser. That surprised Alex that Visser had made and canceled his trip. He called Commander Dupree and told him what he had just learned. Dupree thanked him and wished him a pleasant journey.

Aboard the ship, Alex found the stateroom clean and adequate for the trip to France. Promptly at seven the ship pulled away from the pier into open water. The dinner bell sounded at eight and in a small galley, lobster and shrimp were served with a plentiful supply of wine and other drinks. Finished with his meal, he went out on the deck and stood there for quite some time enjoying the cool breeze and calm sea. Totally contented and relaxed, he retired to his stateroom with thoughts of Sylvia entering his mind. He missed her company and loved her very much. He then fell asleep to the murmur of the ship's engine. Awakened at seven to the sound of the breakfast bell, Alex dressed in a casual sweater and blue slacks for breakfast.

"Thanks for the breakfast," he told the waiter "It was very good." As he was getting ready to leave, a man in his sixties introduced himself as Key Slate, president of a large leather manufacturing company by the name of Mocit. "Have you ever heard of it?"

"No," Alex replied, "but I am part of the LeaBeau Leather Company in France and Morocco. Our companies' process hides at the tanneries for several companies that convert the hides into hats, coats, boots, and many other items."

Key Slate gave him his card and said that he would be in contact with him in the near future.

The ship began to roll from the pounding of the waves as they passed by the Straits of Gibraltar. Alex remembered his father telling him that when he started to get sick he should chew a piece of ginger, swallow some of the bitter juice and in a short time the seasickness would fade.

He hurried down to the kitchen and asked the cook, "Do you have any ginger?"

The cook said "Where did you find out that ginger is good for stopping seasickness?"

Alex said, "My father told me about it when I was a young boy crossing the English Channel."

The cook said, "We always have a supply of ginger for just that reason."

He gave Alex a piece of ginger, which Alex began to chew and swallowed the juices slowly causing the seasickness to stop.

The rest of the trip was uneventful and with the port of Le Havre in view, Alex had the porter bring his luggage to the gangway while the crew was busy unloading the ship. Crowds of people from different countries began to rush to the gangplank trying to make sure that the ship would not leave them behind.

Alex asked a policeman, "Where are all these people going?"

The policeman replied, "This is 1909 and all of these people are going to America to start a new life. They want to escape the poor living conditions and riots over food with the many revolutionary skirmishes in Italy, Germany, France and other parts of Europe. If things do not improve there soon there will be a war of nations. People now are dying by the hundreds because of the violence."

Alex was finding it difficult getting through the crowds to the train station, but after an hour of much pushing and shoving he was able to board the train for Paris. He observed that the train was almost empty of people. And when the conductor came by for Alex to buy his ticket, he asked, "Why is this train almost empty?"

He replied, "Everyone wants to go to America to find work and a better life. You will see how bad it is when you walk through the towns and see no one there except a dog or cat. It is a shame that all my friends are gone," shaking his head as he walked away.

Homecoming

After three hours of train stops, Alex arrived in Paris and had his first ride in a horseless carriage through the streets of Paris. The bumping and rattling sounds from the ride were loud enough to scare people and horses alike, and kept him laughing all the way to the LeaBeau house. The driver helped him with his luggage to the entrance of the home. Claudette, with Rea, came to the front door and wondered what was causing all the noise.

Alex raised both his arms and yelled "I am here, I made it!"

Surprised, they both hugged and kissed him. Claudette looked at Alex saying, "You must be tired, come. We are about ready to have dinner. You must be hungry?"

"Yes I am," he said as they sat down to eat.

The maid and cook told Alex that they missed him and were glad to have him home.

"But he looks thin," Claudette replied, "At least now that he is at home, he can rest anytime he wants to."

They continued to ask questions during dinner about his experience in Casablanca. He told them the details which included recovering stolen hides by the Luster Leather Company and the conviction of its owner, who had also killed one of Commander Dupree's soldiers during his escape from jail. Alex told them that he was still being sought and that his name is Visser, a German.

Rea, tiring of the conversation said, "It is getting late. I am going to bed. We can talk tomorrow morning after breakfast, goodnight."

Claudette told Alex that Rea spent a considerable amount of time talking to Mika on the phone about Alex's progress. She also talked with the manager of the Café Gray Hotel to determine if there were any problems during your stay there. The manager mentioned that you were having an affair with a woman by the name of Sylvia Mundi, who was an investigator from the Justice Department in Paris.

Alex was astounded by all the information that Rea had gathered while he was in Casablanca. "I am amazed that she went through all this to follow my every step, he said.

Claudette said that Rea was concerned that there might be the possibility of harm coming to him and wanted to make sure that he was protected. "I will tell you now that the taxi carriage driver was a highly regarded bodyguard," Claudette added.

"I see it all now," Alex replied, "but I was naïve in thinking that I was accomplishing this alone."

"No questions about Sylvia will come from me," replied Claudette.

A Gift

The following morning after breakfast, Rea offered Alex a half ownership in the three leather companies. The other half would be given to Claudette. She opened a large manila envelope which had been drawn up by her lawyers as a final will, for possession on the home and assets of her companies making them heirs to all her worldly possessions.

"I would like you and Claudette to sign these documents and copies so that I can send the originals promptly to my lawyers."

Claudette questioned Rea, "What is your reason for doing this?"

Her response was that "I am 83 years old and find it more difficult every day to cope with the affairs of the leather companies. Claudette, you have been doing most of the work and Alex has shown me that he has the ability to use good judgment and be an asset to any challenges that might arise."

Claudette agreed and they both thanked Rea for her great generosity.

Rea turned toward Alex, and said, "You have become a well-educated person but I think it would be wise of you to travel in different countries throughout Europe. Are you in agreement with what I said?"

Alex asked "How long will this travel be?"

"A year or more, if my health continues as it is now. People are dying throughout all of Europe from ethnic wars and starvation. Rest until you are ready to leave on your journey. I must, however, emphasize only one condition that you must follow. You must wear ill-fitting clothing, which will not arouse anyone into thinking that you are a wealthy person."

Alex agreed with Rea's suggestion, went shopping and purchased a small amount of cheap clothing for his trip. He said his goodbye to Rea and Claudette.

Leaving France by train, he traveled east to the Poland. There people were starving because of the Russian King Peter's army was stealing their harvested grains and animals for his use and people of favor. He saw vast amounts of people walking carrying what they could to the port city of Ghama. He asked several people why they were leaving their home? The reply from all was the same.

"There is no work and the Russians have stolen our grains and livestock. If you try to stop them the Cossacks will kill you and take everything. They burn our homes. So we are going to America, where we hear that there is work and a better life."

A man approached him with his horse and carriage and asked Alex if he would be kind enough to buy his horse and carriage. He offered it for a very small amount of money which Alex agreed to pay.

In the following weeks he traveled along rural roads through small farming villages. Traveling east and nearing the border of White Russia, he noticed some villagers were still harvesting wheat. Long lines of men were cutting the wheat with their scythes, which women and young children gathered into bundles and hurriedly brought to a designated pile. They continued this process over and over again, throughout the day, cutting, gathering and bundling the wheat.

Suddenly, two women walked hurriedly toward the end of the field where Alex was standing and without taking notice of him standing there one woman, in a kneeling position, gave birth to a baby. Alex slipped through the fence, and was rushing toward the women when the men close to the women shouted at him go away, which Alex did immediately. A third man approached with a shovel and started digging a small deep trench. The woman wrapped the baby in her apron and placed it in the deep trench which was immediately filled with dirt. They all went back to work, including the woman who just had this baby acting as though nothing had happened. Alex could not believe what he had just seen! It was unbelievable to see this happen! It was a horrible experience! It was unbelievable to see what had just happened, a experience he would never forget, repeating) to himself over and over again, "How could anyone do such a horrible thing?"

The evening was getting bitter, with a cold wind that was driving a wet blanket of snow over his horse. Looking for shelter, he noticed a few homes with candlelight shining in the windows. He turned his horse in that direction and arriving there he saw an open shed, large enough to drive his horse into and out of the cold wind. As he stepped down from the inside of his warm, enclosed coach, a man came up to him speaking in Russian and asked, "Who are you and what are you doing here?"

Alex replied in Russian, "I am just visiting your country on my journey through Europe, and I need a bed for the night and some hay for my horse."

The man shouted "You are a Cossack spy! I have no food, only a few rubles. Go away!"

Alex replied, "No, you do not understand. I am not a spy, and here, look at my papers. I am from Paris France."

"I do not read, but I will trust you. If you try to do harm to me or my family, I will kill you. Do you understand?"

Yes, I understand you. May I come in now?"

They entered his house which was built from clay and grass sod. It was one large room with two beds made of straw, a small kitchen with no vent to the outside. A large bucket of horse dung burned in a cast-iron grate above the fire. Overhead was a straw bed where he and his wife slept.

"My son will sleep with my daughter that night and Alex would use his straw bed." In a small area behind the beds there was a stall for a pig, and goat and on the opposite side of the room, a place for their horse and cow.

Alex asked "Why do you keep the animals inside the house?."

"They provide extra heat to keep us warm during the winter months. All the vegetables are in a cold cellar dug underneath the straw beds. When the weather gets colder, I will slaughter the pig for meat, the goat later on if I have to."

Alex was amazed but he still had one question, "When I was some fifteen miles from your home, one of the women working in the field left the group and came over near the fence where she knelt and had a baby, then she then wrapped it in her apron and placed it in a shallow trench that was covered immediately. Why was this done?"

The man replied sadly, "What happened there is commonplace. Her family has too many children. They could not afford to have another child so they quickly bury it and go back to work, trying hard to forget what happened."

Alex, recalling the incident and how horrible it was finally fell asleep only to be awakened by the clatter of the metal pots. He was given a small piece of dark bread and a cup of warm milk, the same as everyone else. Alex gave the man the only rubles left in his pockets. Then was told not to travel east but turn around to head west toward Austria.

The Challenge

Shortly before noon that day Alex stopped by a small stream with ample grass on either side, unhooked his horse and allowed him to graze and drink from the stream for the next few hours. As he was adjusting the hitch and harness to his coach, five Cossack horseman rode up to him. One, looking down at Alex, asked him for his passport papers. While looking at his passport, he asked several questions as to why Alex was in this area?

"I am on a year-long holiday traveling about countries that I have never seen before."

The soldier handed him his papers and without saying a word mounted his horse and all five rode east. Alex continued on. In the late evening, as he approached the town of Schmidtendorf, he noticed a sign pointing east to Vienna, a hundred and ten miles further on. He saw Das Haus, a small inn with a livery stable for his horse. The innkeeper spoke first in German asking "Do you need a room and food?"

"Yes," Alex replied, "also care for my horse. Food first, then you show me where I will sleep".

They brought out a large platter of food and a small plate for him. His wife and daughter with his son all sat down at the table and ate some very tasty food.

Alex asked innkeeper, "Do you take wine with your meals?

"No," he replied, "but I will bring out a bottle of Rhine wine, which was very smooth and of good taste."

After dinner, the innkeeper asked Alex if he could take his daughter to Vienna to spend some time with his brother's family. "She is twenty-five and has never been away from home. This will be good for her."

"Yes, I will take her with me tomorrow and make sure that she gets to your brother's home safely."

The room was comfortable so sleep came immediately. The crowing of a rooster signaled that dawn had arrived. Sitting there with the whole family at breakfast, Alex asked, "What is your daughter's name?"

"It is Besi Ginter and what is your name?"

"It is Alex VanEpp."

"For a Dutchman you speak, very good German. That is good. Besi can read and write in German. She went to school for 6 years."

Alex handed the innkeeper eighty Deutsche Marks.

"That is too much money, fifty marks is enough, thank you."

The horse and the coach were ready for Alex and Besi for their trip to Vienna still three days away. During their trip, Alex questioned Besi as to why she was going to visit her cousin in Vienna?

"I am going to find work and to meet a nice man to marry and have children. It is my desire. There is only work at the inn and there are only a few young men and they spend their free time drinking beer and singing drunken songs. Look at me, am I not a pretty woman?"

"Yes, you are very pretty."

"Then will you marry me? I would make you a good wife, be faithful and have many children."

Alex thought for a moment on what to say without hurting her feelings. He then he told her that he had a lady in Paris who he was going to marry when he returned from this holiday the following spring.

"Besi, be cautious about who you wish to marry. Living with someone that is hateful and dominating in your life can lead to a very bitter end. It will leave you unhappy and lonely. It is a very bad experience."

Besi answered by saying, "That is very good advice. I will always remember what you just said. Thank you Alex."

Grim Warning

After questioning several people to find the address of two-oh-four Linderstrasse, they located the house. Besi introduced herself to her father's brother and wife and their five children, all neatly dressed and clean and about ready to leave for church since this was Sunday, a day of rest. Alex was invited to join them, but he declined by saying maybe the next time. Before leaving, Alex kissed Besi on the forehead and said,

"Will you remember what I told you?"

"Yes and to be sure I will write it down and keep it close to me."

Alex decided to look for a small apartment near the Danube River but received no answer the door. Alex remembered that it was Sunday morning and people were at church. It started to snow and turn bitter cold. Alex thought it was time to visit some of the beautiful old hotels he had seen earlier. He found out immediately that there was no one available to give him a room nor was there any place to eat. It was Sunday and there would be no activity in the restaurants or hotels until six that evening. Walking into a beautiful hotel, Alex had a freedom to choose an overstuffed couch or a large stuffed chair with a foot rest. He removed his shoes and fell asleep on the couch.

A soft nudge from the lady who was the desk clerk roused him.

"Sir, you cannot sleep here. Is that your horse and coach on the street?"

Barely awake, Alex speaking slowly told her he had traveled along way and came into the hotel to rent a room, but found no one, and decided to rest on the couch. "Yes, that is my horse and coach on the street."

She had him come to the desk and signed his request for a room. His horse would be taken to the back of the hotel and put in one of the stables, only as long as he was a guest in this hotel. His luggage was placed by the desk, Alex opened a small satchel that contained his passport and monies from the different countries to which he planned to travel. Removing some German marks he paid for his room and care of the horse.

His room was on the same first level as the restaurant, registration desk and a small bar. He washed quickly, approached the dining room, where a young lady in charge of seating guests told Alex, "Sir, there is no tables left. It is filled with men from the military who have the night off, just a moment, sir."

She left and went into the far corner of the dining room, then quickly returned, telling Alex there is one seat in the in the far corner where three ladies agreed to allow you to dine with them. Alex followed her to the table, where he introduced himself and the women did likewise. He felt uncomfortable with all the German soldiers close by. Sheila, a beautiful blonde woman asked him his full name.

"It is Alex VanEpp."

"You are from Holland? Yes, that is good! If you were from France we would make you pay the whole bill for our dinners", everyone laughed, while she ordered a red wine.

"Alex, what brings you to Vienna?"

"I have been traveling throughout Europe observing how people live and enjoy the fruits of their work."

"What do you think of Austria?"

"I have only been in this beautiful country a short time but I am planning to stay until spring, so maybe then I can give you a better answer."

They agreed to meet on the first of November at the same table at six in the evening. The dining room was nearly empty. When her two friends decided to leave, Sheila told Alex that if he would buy another bottle of wine they could talk and drink in the lounge. Alex agreed, and they both sat down in a small booth with a bottle of wine. She talked about her work as a personal typist for a general who would constantly show his flirtatious manner, touching her breasts and other parts of her body.

"I want a man who is loving, giving and caring. Are you that type of man? Are you Alex?"

"I try to give a woman attention and respect with love and emotion that pleases each person, while being satisfying to both."

Sheila said, "The wine must be twisting my mind, what you just said is the most inviting proposition to sex that I have ever heard. That was a really polite statement. Was it something you remembered from a book that you read or was it from the heart and mind?"

"It was from the emotions on my mind and in my heart."

The bartender came over and told them that it was ten and the service was closing for the night.

Walking from the door, Sheila said, "I am not very steady on my feet, would you help me?"

Alex held her arm. Sheila said, "Will you take me to your room so that I can allow some of this dizziness, to leave my head." Once there, she looked at Alex and said "Can you keep a secret?"

"Yes, of course, I can."

"My father was in the Army a long time ago and served as a diplomat in Ethiopia where he met a tall, beautiful, dark skinned, woman whom he fell in love with. They had one baby some twenty-four years ago and I am that child. The authorities discovered what happened several months later and my father was told to leave the country with me. Upon his return to Austria, he had his widowed sister take care of me as he had lost his commission and pay. The last time I saw him when I was eleven years old. I remember asking my aunt, why doesn't my father come home? She handed me a letter, which stated that he was killed as a soldier in the Greek army. I bleached my hair blonde and bleach my skin to a very light tan and use perfume to cover up the smell of bleach. I know you will not tell anyone; only you and my aunt know my secret. I must go now, I feel much better my mind is now clear and alert. Oh yes, remember, we have a meeting on November 1st at six in the dining room."

Giving Alex a kiss on the cheek, she said, "Thank you for a nice evening, goodnight."

It had been a long evening and Alex, feeling the effects of the wine, quickly fell asleep. Awakened by the brightness of the sun hitting his face, he looked at his watch; the time was nine thirty. He washed, dressed and had breakfast. He told the desk clerk that he planned to stay in Vienna for the winter months and could he have his horse and carriage available in the next half hour. Riding in his carriage, he noticed an abundance of flowers around many of the homes and flower boxes in the windows. No matter where he went about the city, everything was clean, and in its place.

Seeing a gardener, dusting of snow from the flowers, he stopped and asked, "How does everyone keep their flowers looking so pretty in this cold weather?"

The gardener with a smile on his face said, "The flowers are made from small pieces of metal tied together with wire, hand-painted in different colors and placed so everyone can see them all winter."

Alex was amazed by what he had just seen. He passed by a large fenced-in area that was full of military men and material. He stopped to see what they were doing and was immediately confronted by two men in uniform who asked him for his papers.

"Why are you observing the military? What is your business here?"

Alex replied, in perfect German "I am on holiday and not interested in the military, only the beauty of the city."

The soldier spoke to his companion and said he cannot be a spy, he speaks perfect German. "Be on your way! No stopping in this area."

He rode along many side streets finally reaching the main street. He stopped at an outside restaurant and purchased a newspaper which he read during his lunch.

His waitress looked at him and said, "Do you remember me?"

"No, sorry, you do not look familiar."

"I was one of the girls that you had dinner with last night. Your eyes were looking at Sheila that is why you do not remember."

"I will remember you the next time." was his reply.

The winter passed quickly for Alex and his relationship with Sheila was enjoyable when they were together. It was midmorning, when Sheila approached Alex, waiting on the front porch, and said, "I am ready to go wherever you want to take me."

Alex took her down and into his waiting carriage, and suggested the king's garden. "It is very nice, I will guide you there."

The ride was surprisingly quite long, eighteen miles. They toured the Summer Palace, its array of flowers and plants all manicured to perfection. While having lunch, Sheila told Alex that King Wilhelm was no longer there but had been seen at the Royal Palace in Vienna. She went on to say that just before she left on Thursday that the general she worked for, Matt Schnell, had been promoted to the Reich Marshal in full command of all Army operations. Also under his command were Generals Mitter, Spiegel, Weiser and Visser who was new to the group. From what she had typed only Visser was in charge of collecting spy intelligence. The others, all members of the Palace courts, had duties with the Army.

Alex wondered to himself if Visser was the same man that had killed one of Commander Dan Dupree's soldiers during the investigation of stolen animal hides at the LeaBeau Leather Company in Casablanca? Sheila also told him that there were photographs taken of the five generals and she would try to obtain a print for him to see.

They had dinner at a small restaurant a few miles from the King's Palace. Darkness had fallen during dinner so Alex inquired if there were any sleeping quarters in the area? The innkeeper said they had several small cottages available with horse shelters.

Looking at Sheila, Alex said, "Would you like to spend the night here?"

"Yes of course, yes",

The horse was led to the shelter and given hay and water. Alex and Sheila went into the small cottage which was warm and comfortable, with two oil lamps emitting a soft yellow glow to the room. There was a bottle of wine already open with two glasses, inviting them to drink. During the evening they danced to the music on the phonograph. The Blue Danube Waltz and the taste of wine soon made their rhythm unsteady.

"I think it is time to stop dancing?" Alex said as he sat down.

"Mmm, not yet", Sheila said drowsily. The kerosene lamps gave Alex enough light to start the record of the Blue Danube again.

When Sheila placed her arms around Alex she said, "Dance with me."

Together they drank their wine and danced until the rhythm aroused their emotions and they made love into the early hours of the morning. At ten, they decided to not have breakfast but instead they would ride along a road by the Blue Danube River for the rest of the day.

By late afternoon, they saw a beautiful hotel overlooking the Danube, Sheila asked, "Can we stay at that hotel this night?"

"We'll see if they have a room with a view of the river," was his answer.

Checking in at the hotel, the clerk asked about their luggage, "We have none," They laughed together. Their room was large and comfortable with a balcony that gave a wide review of the Danube and the surrounding area.

Sheila responded with a radiant, smile, "Alex, this room is just perfect. I have some money to help pay for the room. It must be very expensive."

"No. I have enough money to cover the expenses."

They ordered an early dinner and ate out on the balcony sipping from a bottle of wine sent with compliments from the hotel. They continued to dine while the sun was setting in the west. Soon a cool breeze urged them into the warmth of the room set with a crackling fire. Two waiters removed the dinner setting on the balcony then closed the two large glass doors at the balcony's entrance.

Sheila standing at the bathroom door called to Alex, "Come here and see this."

Alex entered the bathroom, and Sheila pointed to the tub. "It's very large with plenty of room for two people. I will fill it with warm water for us to enjoy."

The warm water was very relaxing, and the pleasure of joining in love made time melt away. A warm shower with perfumed soapy bubbles covering both of them created a strong desire to continue their passionate love with one another. Dried and exhausted, they fell asleep with her arms encircling one another.

The following morning, they dressed, had breakfast, after which Alex pay a sizable amount for the room, food and services, also leaving a sizable tip for those that served them. The rest of the day was spent viewing parts of the city and surrounding area. Stopping at a small tavern they both enjoyed a light meal with an apple strudel dessert and a warm cup of coffee.

Alex asked Sheila, "Now tell me where you live so I can take you home."

Sheila replied, "No. I must take a carriage home alone. There are so many people following the movements of those working for the military. There is a surveillance team that follows me some of the time. Next week, I will meet you here at this small tavern on Wednesday at six."

She stepped from the carriage and walked down the street and boarded another carriage that took her away.

Alex spent the next three days, concerned about Sheila's well-being. since she was with him. He was after all a foreigner, who in their eyes would be considered a spy looking for information about the military.

The weather had turned cold and an unusual light snow was falling as he approached the tavern of their last meeting. He entered the restaurant and found no one at the tables. Looking at his watch, he noticed the time to be seven. He ordered hot coffee and sat there wondering where Sheila was? Finally at eight she walked in to the restaurant and quickly over to where Alex was sitting.

"What happened? Why are you so late?"

"Please order dinner and I will tell you what happened at the general's session today. The generals had their photos taken Tuesday morning, and I took notes of their meetings that day until six. I spent most of the evening typing what was said and by whom. This morning I went to the office early to go over what I had typed. General Schnell came in the office at nine, read the pages of the meeting and asked if the photographer had delivered any photographs? I told him no photographs had been delivered. Then almost immediately after that had been said, the photographs arrived. General Schnell was pleased with the pictures, and as he walked toward his office he said to me, How many photographs are there? I need twelve. I had counted fourteen and the one he had taken made fifteen.

A Perfect Match

General Schnell wanted an additional sixteen so I went to the photographer and gave him the order of the General's request. On the table, there were several prints of the generals which he said they had slight blemishes and were going to be thrown away along with others in the wastepaper basket. As he was working I took these two photographs, which you can now have."

Alex looked at the photographs and immediately recognized Visser's face, "This is the man I am looking for! Thank you Sheila, this is very important to me."

They finished dinner and as they were leaving the restaurant she rolled her fur collar up to a point on her face making her eyes barely visible. As they rode away in a carriage Sheila told Alex that they are planning a war to invade Poland, Russia, France and several of the smaller nations in the year of 1912 or 1913. She also told Alex that she could no longer see him because of the spies in the military our observing everyone's movements. It had to be good bye.

"I love you, and I will miss you forever."

They approached an empty carriage and she hurriedly stepped in and waved as she rode away disappearing into the falling snow.

Alex arrived at his hotel at midnight. He left his horse and carriage in the shelter and went to his room without seeing anyone. He felt empty and lonely inside. He had no doubt that he had fallen in love with Sheila and would miss her very much. He told the desk clerk that he would be leaving that morning. The desk clerk replied that his horse was fed, watered, brushed dry then covered with a horse blanket, which you could buy if you wished. Alex agreed to the purchase and a short time later he started on his journey back to Paris.

On the third day of his trip, his horse lost one of its shoes. Seeing a railroad station close by with a livery stable behind, he stopped and asked the ticket master for directions on how to get to Paris?

"This train was going through Brussels, Belgium and from there you could board a train for Paris."

Alex bought his ticket for Brussels and took the horse and carriage to the livery stable. No one seemed to be in the working shed or barn. Alex saw no horses on the premises. Finally, a muscular woman emerged from a fenced gate, shouting, "What is your business here?"

Alex replied, "My horse lost a shoe. Is there anyone here that can replace it?"

"It will not take some time to do that work."

Alex said, "I do not see any horses in your yard."

She snapped back an angry tone and said "Those miserables came here last week and took all twenty-two horses for the army. I have nothing left but a cow and some chickens. They paid me for what they took, but what good is the money if I do not have any horses."

"Would like to buy my horse and carriage?"

After carefully inspecting the horse, each hoof and all other parts of the carriage, she offered Alex a price that was higher than what he had paid for its original sale. The train arrived in the early evening. Once on board he sat down and had an acceptable meal. Arriving in Brussels in the early morning hours, he fell asleep in the depot while waiting for the ticket office to open. Alex awoke to find the station busy with the sounds of people talking and small children screaming. He purchased his ticket for Paris and with little time left boarded the train crowded with passengers. He pressed his way toward the dining car where he was able to sit with three male passengers who all introduced themselves.

Then they asked Alex, "Where do you live?"

"In France", was his response.

"Where in France?" they queried.

Alex became annoyed by the questioning and to fend off further questioning, said, "I am looking for a residence somewhere in the outskirts of Paris. From there I will look for work as a teacher of languages."

They responded by telling him that there were joining in the French Foreign Legion. "Join us and we will go to Algeria!"

"Not for now", Alex replied, "I have other plans."

Arriving in Paris that morning, Alex said goodbye to his three companions and boarded a taxi for his ride to his great grandmother's house. It was Saturday morning, and stepping from the taxi he was greeted by the gardener. With his help they took his luggage into the house where he found Claudette and Rea having breakfast. Both were surprised at seeing him.

"Come have breakfast. You must be hungry."

Alex sat down and began to eat a stack of French toast with syrup and coffee.

"You have been away a long time and it is nice to have you home for the holidays. Christmas will soon be here, and then the New Year of 1913."

Rea said "Alex, tell us about your travels. You been gone a year and a half and your letters were very brief and not too often, I might say."

Alex spent the next hours telling them of his travels and the concern he had about the Germans preparing for war against France and some of the smaller surrounding nations. He also showed them a picture of the German generals and pointed out in a photo a picture of Visser, who was involved in the theft of animal hides from the LeaBeau Leather Company and the killing of one Commander Dupree's soldiers.

"I will call the commander and tell him where Visser can be found. While in Vienna, I met a beautiful girl with whom I had spent many happy hours. That is a long story and someday I will tell you more about her. Now tell me, what is going on with both of you and how are they companies doing?"

Claudette spoke up saying, "Rea, no longer goes to the office. I discuss the operations with her each evening and she helps me in making decisions that keeps all the operations in control. She is now eight-five years old and needs her rest. Business has been very good, and profits well above expectations. We have agreed to give all the employees extra money for Christmas with a holiday from Christmas to one day after the New Year."

"That is a wonderful gift, what a surprise for everyone. I am sure they will all appreciate what is being done for them. And it is going to be paid back by their efforts in the future."

News of Visser

With the holidays and gift giving time that had just passed, Alex looked forward to working with Claudette on the operations. It felt good to be responsible for the decisions that he would make with Claudette's approval. In early April he received a letter with no return address. Inside was a newspaper article stating that fishermen found a body in the shallows and towed it to shore. Visser's body was found on the shore of Lake Laurel, apparently a victim of accidental drowning. The overturned boat resting close by confirmed what had happened. Alex looked at the postmark which showed that it had been mailed from Berlin. He placed the envelope with the newspaper clipping into the wood-burning stove and watched it burst quickly into a flame.

The local newspaper printed an extra copy that a attempt to assassinate King Wielheim of Austria failed. The assassin was a French loyalist who was apprehended a short time later then killed by members of the Kings guard. It also stated by Matt Schnell, that this attempt on the King was a cowardly attack with grave consequences to the nations that caused the incident.

A Proposition

Alex found very little time to enjoy the fruits of his work. Claudette urged him to take some holiday time but he felt that would include a heavier workload on her. At one of their meetings with a leather buyer Alex was introduced to a beautiful woman by the name of Lee Bisset. Lee had stores throughout the world selling leather goods for men and women, with a standard of high quality and of course a very high price. The meeting lasted until lunch. When both buyers and sellers sat down to have lunch, Alex made a point of sitting directly opposite Lee Bisset who was insisting on having contracts that would give her an ample supply of hides for her business. Alex replied that they could not allow a commitment that would possibly curtail shipments to the small companies that have always been loyal to the company.

Lunch was over and as everyone was turning to leave, Lee turned to Alex and said, "I would like to discuss this a little further. Could we meet for dinner at seven at the Fountain Hotel?"

"I will be there at seven." was his response.

On the way home, Claudette told Alex to be careful, That she-cat has sharp claws that will never let you go."

Arriving at the hotel a few minutes before seven, he approached the table where Lee was sitting. "Your punctual appearance gives you a high mark for your presence."

"I have always tried to be on time, regardless of the appointment I was having."

Lee had several questions to ask Alex. "Do you have a girlfriend or a mistress? Are you married? Do you have a male lover?"

"My response to all your questions is a definite no."

"Then my guess is that you cannot satisfy a woman with your lovemaking. Is my guess right?"

Alex with a large grin on his face, said, "I have not been asked this many personal questions in my life. I feel like a fugitive being questioned by a detective."

Lee said "I am sorry, but I just forgot and thought I was questioning a future employee for my company. Alex please accept my apology, it certainly was a wrong way to start."

Dinner was slow with more wine than food being consumed. Lee was impressed with his background in several languages and his quiet and polite demeanor. Without Alex asking, she told him of being the youngest of six children born into a poor family whose father worked in a woolen mill and the mother took in laundry.

"With barely enough money to put food on the table they both passed away before I reached the age of sixteen and I was taken away by my church to a convent, where I learned to make designs on leather handbags. I never made any money from my work, room and board was considered payment enough. At nineteen I left the convent and went to college in the town of Le Harve Mori where I worked as an evening waitress and did laundry for the local people. I continued to design leather handbags. After graduating from college, I continued designs on leather which had become a very profitable business. That is when I decided to start leather retail stores throughout the world with my trademark LeeB."

They talked about their lives until they were reminded that the dining room was closing for the evening. They started to walk away when she stopped to say, "Thank you Alex for a nice evening. Walk me to my door?"

"Of course I will."

Lee opened the door and invited Alex into her room where he immediately noticed a bottle of wine being chilled in a ice bucket with two glasses placed nearby. Lee told Alex to take off his coat and relax as she left to change into something more comfortable and alluring. She reappeared in a revealing nightdress that caused Alex to stare. The wine left a pleasant taste on the palate and the tray of assorted hors d'oeuvres were delicious. Lee turned on a small radio that was sending out soft French music which Alex prompted Alex to ask Lee, "Do you dance?"

"Not very well, but I will try."

While in their dancing embrace Alex noticed that her body was pressing firmly to his waist. The kissing and foreplay became more intense and continued on in the bedroom with Lee's strong desire to make love with Alex. They enjoyed these satisfying moments until the early hours of the morning. They showered and dressed promising each other that they would meet whenever possible during the next five months. And they did meet, time and time again to enjoy the pleasures of one another.

A Difficult Decision

On a late evening in May, Alex had just left the office and found a taxi waiting for him, which seemed very unusual. He thought it might be Lee Bisset but instead he found two men urging him to step inside the cab. He was quickly told that they worked for the government and were taking him to a special building.

Upon arrival, he was introduced to Inspector Armin, who then took him to an adjoining room with comfortable chairs and a variety of food on a coffee table. He stated that one reason for this meeting was to see if Alex would, for his country, become an agent in espionage and arrange termination of certain individuals preparing to start a war against France and several other countries.

"We are aware of your background in language at Oxford University," he began, "Also, your ability to dedicate yourself to helping others. If after our discussions here, you decide that you are not interested in this case then I remind you to not divulge any of this information with anyone. You are well aware that Germany's generals are eager to conquer through war, at any cost, to any nation that stands in their way. The Generals that must be eliminated are Schnell, Mitter, Spiegel, and Weisser. Before I go any further I need a commitment from you here and now. What I will continue to tell you is highly classified. I need your answer, yes or no?"

Alex said, "How long do you expect this project will last?"

"I can only answer you by saying it could last two years or more. Any letters that you will write to your mother will go to this address and we will deliver to your mother, Claudette. She in turn will send her letters to this address and we will deliver her letters to you. Our agents are all committed to the freedom of France. The three hundred mile line of trenches on France's northern border to Germany will not be adequate in stopping the spearhead of Germany's elite army and tanks. It is also rumored that they have a large supply of deadly gas that would kill men by the thousands. What is your answer Alex VanEpp?"

"My answer is yes, I will do everything that I possibly can to lessen the chance of war or eliminate those who are the aggressors."

The Plan

Alex was taken and the next room that contained engineers and chemists working on a variety of projects. He was introduced to a gentle, gray-haired man in his mid-forties whose name was Pitor.

"Pitor is a magician in repairing and using different types of cameras, he will be your shadow in every action that might occur. He has a strong hate for the Germans. They destroyed his family home on the Hungarian border, killing his family and his parents, two very old people who were locked in his house and then set on fire. Come into my office, I will discuss the contents of this plan with you."

Inspector Armin outlined the steps Alex was to take.

"Number 1. You are to shave your head bald, grow a mustache and beard. You should use heavy and dark rimmed eyeglasses, unmatched clothing with German discarded shoes. This will all be done by the time you arrive here for your next meeting.

Number 2. The photographer working in the general's compound is scheduled for a vacation to Hot Springs in Cortina, Italy. He will be apprehended when he changes trains at Berne, Switzerland. Transported by automobile, he will be confined to our special prison for as long as hostilities last. You will receive new credentials and passport photos showing you bearded and bald with a new name, Luke Zeiger. This will create the opportunity.

Number 3. Pitor and you will take his cameras and other equipment to General Schnell's compound where you will inform the General's orderly that you are photographers in search of work. You have no idea as to the whereabouts or the name of their photographer. You present your forged credentials and passports to the orderly. I am sure the general will hire you as photographers as he likes to have his picture taken all the time; his ultra-ego never stops. In two months your beard should be long enough for your passport photograph, your head will be shaved and you must keep it shaved clean."

Every week Alex was escorted from the building to a waiting taxi which took him to his office the leather company as it did many times before. The driver was a secret agent from the intelligence office. In the following weeks Claudette noticed that Alex was displaying a beard which made him look more impressive.

She asked Alex, "What made you decide to grow a beard?

"I just got tired of shaving every morning."

"You look very distinguished," was Claudette's reply.

Midway through the third month, the papers and radio brought news that King Wilhelm had been assassinated and the assassin, presumed to be a French loyalist, had not been apprehended. Alex leaving the office boarded a taxi for the ride home. The driver explained who he was, then telling Alex that his part in the project was complete. Alex was to meet the following morning at eight with an intelligence agent who would drive him to the office of Inspector Armin.

"Ask the taxi driver for the password to which he should reply with the word Bonaparte."

That evening, news of the assassination interrupted normal programming with the final news item that Germany had declared war on several nations including France, which they indicated was the perpetrators of the King's assassination.

A Surprising Plot

Alex told Claudette that he was going to join the service and defend France against Germany and any other country hostile to France. He hated to leave her with the burden of controlling the interests of the three leather companies. Claudette responded that their more than enough competent people to continue the operations and control of the company's assets. She asked Alex to write often and she promised to reply to every letter that she received.

Alex did not sleep well that night. He tossed and turned and by six he was dressed and went to the kitchen for breakfast. Claudette and Rea followed a few minutes later. There was no talk about Alex's decision to join the service. Alex hugged and kissed both of them, promising to write often. He then left without taking any personal items. Before entering the cab, Alex asked for the password. The taxi driver responded with the word 'Bonaparte'.

They drove to a building where a large door was opened and the driver entered a large open room. Stepping out of the car, Alex was escorted by two men to The Inspector's office where a barber stood ready to cut his hair and shave his head. The Inspector gave Alex a mirror and asked him, "Do you know this man?"

"My name is Luke Zeiger."

"Now Luke, Zeiger come with me." They entered a room called FINAL.

"This is where we deal with the methods of eliminating persons sabotaging or killing persons from our country. I will only explain what you are to do. If you have any questions during my explanation, interrupt if you wish."

Secret Death

He was shown a wire cage that held a big black snake and was told it was a Black Mamba from Africa.

"This is one of the top ten most venomous snakes in the world. Two drops in a person's body would kill in three hours."

They walked over to a table, where Armin explained another small lethal weapon that could kill. What Alex saw was a small crossbow, a half inch wide with a slotted tube and a crossbow one and a quarter inches wide, able to fire a projectile at fifty miles per hour. Inspector Armin opened a case that held vials and sixteen hypodermic needles attached to a plunger that forced the poison into the needle.

"Notice that the area between the vial and the needle has compression rings that slide over the needle, so that when the needle enters the skin the needle and vial are ejected from the skin and fall to the ground. You can crush it or dispose it any way to avoid suspicion."

Alex observed silently.

"Alex, the cross bow, must be strapped to your left hand above the wrist with three thin wires supporting your coat above the crossbow. A thin wire that has been attached to the trigger of the crossbow follows the line of the needle to the middle finger of your left hand where you will attach it to this adjustable ring. You are to point your finger toward the back of the persons head just above his hairline, move your fingers into a fist position and the crossbow and dart will do the rest. Do not forget to crush or retrieve the spent vial. I suggest that you practice, the operation of the crossbow. It could save your life," he finished solemnly.

An agent entered with a message for The Inspector. "I have received word that General Matt Schnell's photographer is in our custody. When we have him in a permanent lockdown, I will let you know. Then you and Pitor will be able to travel to the general's headquarters and interview to replace his photographer."

Alex was having trouble responding to the name Luke Zeiger, but after several days he responded to the name quickly. His accuracy with the poison dart improved a hundred percent, up to a distance of ten feet.

On the eighth day, he and Pitor were given a substantial amount of German marks and note detailing travel routes.

"Take a ferry boat from Cannes to Copenhagen, spend one night there then take a train from Denmark to Bern, Germany and by train to Vienna, Austria. A half mile from the train station on Strasbergstrasse is number seventy-one. It is a small two bedroom with a kitchenette and washing facilities. This will be your home for a long time unless your true identity is discovered. Be very certain that all of your tickets from traveling are disposed of immediately by burning. Good luck on defeating the challenges that await you. Burn this note NOW!!"

Deception

Pitor and Luke traveled according to the instructions in the letter, arriving as Strasbergstrasse seventy-one in the late evening. They immediately went shopping for food and beer. Luke also bought a bottle of German wine. That evening Luke shaved his head and while looking in a mirror he found it difficult to identify his face as he once knew it. Only his voice had the same sound. It was at that moment that he recalled that Sheila, who he willingly loved very much, was a secretary to General Matt Schnell. He hoped that he would not see her and he would be careful to avoid her at all times.

The following day they went to the Army civilian employment office. They filled out the necessary papers and their occupation. As they sat there waiting to be called, they noticed trucks filled with soldiers leaving the headquarters for duty on the Western front. Their names were called and they were assigned to a very young orderly who took them to the headquarters of the General. Entering the door to the general's office Luke saw Sheila and he immediately turned his head so that she would not recognize him. The General's orderly motioned them to follow him to General Matt Schnell's room where after a brief discussion about their qualifications and a notebook of photographs was presented, he immediately offered them the position of being his personal photographer. The orderly would see that they were outfitted with German army uniforms and documents verifying their position.

They went to the Army Depot and were given underwear, clothing and new leather boots with a trademark from the Luster Leather Company and a bag containing their civilian clothing. They marched to their apartment pleased by their progress. Luke sat down and wrote a short letter to Claudette avoiding all information about where he was or what he was doing. He had been given an address to send his letters in the town of Berg where someone would then forward the letter to Claudette.

Dart of Death

Luke seemed unmoved by his plans for assassinating the four generals. Mitter, who was in charge of the movement of supplies to the front, was his first choice. He was a young, arrogant person that enjoyed giving orders, drinking and having women in his presence at the local bars. Luke felt the end of 1914, would be a good time to dart him.

In the evening before the New Year, Luke with Pitor looked in several bars for Mitter and finally found him in a drunken stupor with two ladies-of-the-evening. Luke suggested that they take him to his room which they did while he stumbled along. As they were unlocking the door, Luke looked up and down both sides of the hallway and seeing no one raised his left hand toward the back of Mitter's head and clenched his fist. A moment later, Luke saw the vial and dart near his shoe. He picked it up, avoiding the point and carefully put it in his coat pocket. With Pitor at his side they hurriedly left the building through the back door. Back to their apartment, Luke removed the vial and dart from his coat pocket and saw that the vial was empty of poison. He placed the vial between two bricks and crushed it onto a small piece of paper then he discarded it into their coal burning stove.

One Down

Three days had gone by, and Luke had heard nothing about Mitter's condition wondering if the poison really worked? On the fifth day a memo from General Matt Schnell arrived.

"News arrived to him that General Mitter was in a motor accident two days prior to this announcement and was pronounced dead at the scene. A terrible loss, he will be missed by everyone."

It was late July when they received transfer orders stating they would be spending the remainder of the year taking photographs of the generals and soldiers in the trenches fighting the French. Luke knew that General Spiegel was in charge of the big guns and their placement toward the enemy lines. Also, German soldiers were becoming, very sick caused by the lack of toilet facilities and mud in the trenches. Luke noticed Sheila kissing General Matt Schnell. Then as she walked away he noticed that she was pregnant. Luke did not blame her for finding someone else. It is had been several months since their last affair so not being recognized by her gave him a sigh of relief.

Arriving at the front lines, General Matt Schnell ordered photographs be taken of the generals and the soldiers as quickly as possible. The rumble of guns and rifle fire seemed to continue nonstop until night fall, only to start again as the sun began to rise in the eastern sky. The new year 1916 came with a blast of cold temperatures and snow. Scattered smoke from cigarettes in the trenches attracted gunfire by both armies. In June of 1916 General Matt Schnell decided to go back to Vienna to explain the progress of the war to the ministers and what was needed to obtain victory.

Luke and Pitor were replacing photographic film and developing chemicals for the next trip to the front when he noticed Sheila carrying a black child. Luke made a dash for the developing room and peering through a small slot in the door. He watched her enter the room with a black baby in her arms.

Pitor asked Sheila, "Who is the mother of that baby?"

"I am. He is a beautiful black boy. I wish the man I loved very much, could see him. He knew that I was born of mixed blood; my father German and my mother, Ethiopian. Where is your partner Luke?"

"He is in the darkroom developing photographs and cannot open the door until he has finished, I will tell him you were here."

Sheila left with her boy heading back to the generals office. Luke did not expect to see Sheila with a black child and attributed its color to her parents of mixed blood.

In the fall of 1916 Luke and Pitor were ordered back to the front lines of battle. With fierce winds and waist deep snow, the fighting had come a standstill. In April of 1917, several railroad tanker cars with the identifying mark of a skull and cross bones arrived at the Central command posts along with many trucks that started distributing gas masks.

Luke asked one of the soldiers arriving with the railroad cars, "What is happening?"

"General Spiegel had been informed that Germany is losing the war and this material in the tank cars is called mustard gas. I saw it used on animals in Stuttgart and they died in a very short time."

Luke noticed swarms of bees pollinating the fruit trees and flowers that surrounded the small farm where Spiegel's command posts were. Luke decided General Spiegel had to be killed before he gave any orders to use the deadly gas. He found a beehive in the orchard and carrying a small box with sugar placed it in one small hole. He waited for the bees to enter the box and then placed a piece of tape over the hole. With their camera equipment and the box of bees they went to see General Spiegel, who was outlining plans for the distribution of the poison gas to his staff.

Luke prepared his left hand with a crossbow and vial of poison in Spiegel's restroom. Prior to taking a photograph, they inspected Spiegel's appearance and Luke placed a small amount of sugar water on the back of his collar. Then he carefully opened the box. Within moments the bees began flying directly to the back of Spiegel's collar, who began to yell and flap his arms.

"Get these bees away from me! Hurry do something!"

Luke pointed his left hand at the back of Spiegel's head, clenched his fist and a moment later the vial dropped to the floor. Luke quickly retrieved it also crushing the small box and placed it in with their camera equipment. The orderly arrived with a doctor who examined the bee stings, gave Spiegel's some ointment, telling him the pain would not last long. Spiegel canceled the staff meeting, and spent the following day in bed. On the following day, his orderly, found him dead. The doctor wrote a memo that the cause of death was due to several bees stings to which General Spiegel was allergic.

General Weisser, next in command, went into Spiegel's planning room and gathered up all the plans for dispersing the poisonous gas. He immediately had his men start filling the empty canisters with the liquid gas. A short time later he was informed that the men filling the canisters were choking and dying. He ordered that the men filling the canisters to wear gas masks. "Dumkofs!"

Trucks took loads of filled canisters to the German trenches where the soldiers waited for the wind to blow toward the French and allied troops. Then they opened the canisters and watched the yellow gas slowly creep along the ground into the French trenches where the coughing and screaming of dying men could be heard. Over the next week thousands of men died this way and the Germans cheered that soon the war would be over. On many other occasions the wind direction would change blowing the lethal gas back into the German trenches, killing hundreds that were not wearing gas masks.

Luke had to find some way to stop General Weisser from using this lethal gas. He and Pitor were to take photographs inside a tunnel complex found by the Germans. Luke instructed Pitor to take flash photographs near the general while he would position himself behind, the general and be able to shoot his poisonous vial.

They entered the dark tunnel, disturbing hundreds of bats which caused everyone into trying to hide themselves from the fluttering wings. With the flash bulbs going off every few minutes

Luke positioned himself behind the general who was trying to calm the men. He raised his hand toward the back of the generals head, clenched his fist and in a moment the empty poisonous dart dropped to the ground. Luke could hardly see it in the dark surroundings but a flash of light from Pitor's camera enabled him to pick up the vial and place it in his pocket. The general never responded to the piercing of the needle on the back of his head.

Everyone left the tunnel, returning to their private quarters. The next day General Weisser was active, giving commands to his staff. On the third day, he collapsed during a ride to a poisonous gas distribution point where he was pronounced dead by a highly respected doctor who announced that he had inhaled a large amount of poisonous gas. The use of the poisonous gas was discontinued in the coming months of 1917. The Germans surrendered to the French and allied armies.

Three Down, One To Go

Pitor and Luke left by train for Vienna and it was during that trip Pitor asked Luke. "Why are you so determined to kill General Matt Schnell?"

"My orders were to eradicate four generals and he is the fourth one on my list."

"But the war is over. Do you have many sleepless nights?"

"Those generals being dead, means nothing to me. They flirted with death and lost." Luke asked Pitor, "Don't you hate those that killed your family?"

"No. What is done is done, I try to forget and live without hate which destroys the mind into a fitful existence."

They stopped by the apartment long enough to retrieve minor items that had been left during their trips to the front. Luke opened a letter from Claudette that had been lying there for several months. It had some sad news. Rea had passed away after a long struggle with pneumonia. Claudette wished that he could have been by Rea's side when she passed away.

Luke destroyed all his forged documents, shaved his beard, combed his hair and dressed in his civilian clothing. He destroyed by fire the crossbow and vials of poison. He now was no longer Luke Zeiger of the German army but Alex VanEpp, a resident of France. He had decided that killing General Matt Schnell served no purpose and should be forgotten. He entered the headquarters and immediately noticed Sheila and her dark skinned child.

As he walked toward her she recognized Alex saying, "Alex, my Alex, what a wonderful surprise to see you again. This is my young son and yes, you are his father. I had no one to turn to when I realized that I had become pregnant. So I had a romantic affair with the general who was deeply in love with me. Yes, the General and I were secretly married soon after he was born. He will always be your son and when I look at him. I will be reminded of the love we once shared. My son's name is Brent Schnell. Remember his name for someday you might meet him again. Matt has taken very good care of us, and we plan to go to Spain after his discharge from the Army."

Alex was completely surprised by what Sheila had done and pleased that he had taken no action on terminating General Matt Schnell's life. Good things were happening. He introduced himself to the general and was invited to dinner at the Palace Restaurant where Alex had to fend off questions about his whereabouts during the war.

The general looking into Alex's eyes said, "You look very familiar. I am sure I have seen you many times before. Are you sure we have not met?"

Alex replied, "No. I was in Paris the whole war working with my mother on the operation of our leather manufacturing companies."

Dinner ended with a farewell and hopes of happiness for the General, Sheila and their son.

Despair

Knowing that he had lost Sheila and he was the father of her son, Alex troubled his mind to a point that he became very despondent and aimlessly walked the streets of Vienna. Unable to make decisions about returning to Paris and his mother Claudette, he went to the intelligence headquarters for his passport and final report.

It had been four years and Alex now thirty-five could see no purpose in doing anything except having a deep remorse about assassinating three generals. After two weeks of deliberating with himself he decided to go home to Paris and his mother Claudette. New clothing for his trip gave him a good feeling and an urgency to travel.

Now with ticket in hand, he boarded the night train at eleven for his trip to Paris. It was a seven hour trip and Alex felt that he would be home in time to have breakfast with Claudette. After a few hours, Alex fell asleep in his cushioned seat. In what seemed like a short time, he was awakened by the conductor, who told him they had arrived in Paris, on time. It was six in the morning and since Alex had no luggage he immediately gave the taxi driver his home address as they left the train station.

Arriving at home he noticed that the home, with its flower garden's had not changed in the five years that he was gone. As he entered the hallway, he saw Claudette coming down the stairs holding tightly onto the railing, shouting all my heavens.

"Alex, Oh, Alex, it is you?" As she began to cry, he hurried to her arms and quietly said,

"I am home to stay. I miss you very much and wondered at times why you did not write but I knew you would be here when I returned."

They went into the kitchen for breakfast where the cook and maid were happy to see Alex alive and well. During their meal, Claudette asked Alex.

"Why did not you answer any of my letters that I sent to you. A lawyer in the investigating court system asked where you might be reached. I told her that I not heard from you in the last four years. I did not think it right to give her your address in Vienna. She left me a business card that I kept, and it is next to the phone."

Alex found Sylvia's card. "I will plan to see her in the near future."

He then told Claudette all his activities and undercover assignments he had when he worked as a espionage agent for the intelligence office. Alex did not wish to tell Claudette that he was involved in the assassination of three German generals during the war. They spent the remainder of the day talking about Rea, the leather companies and those involved in its manufacture.

Claudette also mentioned "Lee Bisset had been stopping in her office asking about your whereabouts. Did I have an address she could write a letter to? I told her that I had not received any letters from you. I have not seen or heard from her in the past two years. She did mention that if I had any thought about selling the Paris Company, she would be interested in buying it. I know she left a card with her address and telephone number. I think it is in my reference file at the office."

During the next several days, Alex and Claudette discussed the business of the leather companies, where they had been and what they had done. Claudette's time was used in controlling the business and spending her spare time taking care of Rea by making her final months pleasant. Alex talked about his role in the intelligence service and what he had accomplish but never telling her of his assassin role or fathering a black child in Vienna.

New Surprises

Alex left one morning for Inspector's Armin's office to retrieve his real passport and other identification papers. Inside the entrance he was stopped by a security agent who was sitting behind his desk.

He asked Alex, "What is your business?"

"I am here to see Inspector Armin."

"Your passport and papers?" said the officer.

"My passport and other personal papers are with The Inspector," replied Alex.

"What is your name?"

"My name is Alex VanEpp."

The agent looked through the files for several minutes then quietly looked up at Alex and said, "Your name is not in our files, and I cannot give you a day pass to see anyone."

Frustrated Alex wrote a note to Inspector Armin, telling him who he was and why he wanted to see him. A very young agent took his note and disappeared down a long hallway. One hour had passed before this young agent appeared at the desk. He began talking to the agent and pointing to Alex, who motioned him to come to the desk. The agent gave him a day pass.

"We have strict security that we must follow."

The young agent took Alex to Inspector Armin's office and left. A few minutes went by when the inspector entered his office with an assistant carrying a wooden box with a latch and lock.

"It is good to see you Alex or should I call you Luke. I had been informed that you had died of poison gas at the front lines in Germany. You solved a lot of problems by being alive. Now I do not have to tell your mother of your death. This box contains all your important papers that you left here four years ago. There are also letters written by your mother which we kept to keep your identity secure. Eliminating the three generals created chaos in the movement of troops and the use of poisonous gas. You saved thousands of lives because no one else in the German command wanted the responsibility of using poisonous gas in the front lines."

Alex retrieved his papers. "Thank you. I was proud to serve the French army."

The Inspector continued, "I never mentioned that there was a price on each of the German generals. We know that three of them died in accidents or non-suspicious deaths. You were not aware that there was a hundred thousand dollar reward for every general that died. If you had not returned in the next five years, the money totaling three hundred thousand dollars would have been given to your mother. In this box, you will find the name of the Swiss bank where we have deposited your money and the security code numbers for its withdrawal. The reason for payment in American dollars was to avoid any connection that could be made to the French government's involvement in the deaths of the German generals."

Alex was shocked and surprised at all of the unknowns being answered. He thanked the inspector who handed him a key that would open the lock. Leaving by a side door, Alex placed the box in the back seat of a taxi and not even giving directions soon found himself at the front door of his home. With box in hand, he went directly to his bedroom. Then called Claudette to come into his bedroom to show her what he had. As she entered, Alex was opening the box which was full of neatly tied bundles of letters from Claudette and one letter from Alex to Claudette. A complete history of where he had been in the past four years and what he had done. The Swiss bank passbook with three hundred dollars on account was for the services he had provided.

Unknown Family History

After hours of reading some letters and notes they decided to store the box in the closet. Claudette with a surprised look on her face turned to Alex and said, "Just a minute. Do not go away. I just remembered something."

She left the bedroom and returned in a very short time, carrying a metal case with the letters inscribed on the top "Personal Property of Astin VanEpp". Claudette told Alex that a short time after selling their home on the French Riviera this metal case arrived here at this house with a letter that it had been found behind a kitchen cabinet.

"I had completely forgotten about that that metal case until now. When we were looking through your papers, it reminded me of this metal case."

Alex looked at the case, and asked Claudette. "Do you have the combination to unlock this case?"

Claudette said, "I think that I know where it might be." Again, she left the room. Waiting for over an hour, Alex decided go to Claudette's bedroom and see what had happened to her.

Finding her surrounded by papers, letters and notepads Alex said, "I can see that you have not found what you are looking for?"

"It is here, I know it is here, but I just cannot find it."

"I will help you find it, do you have any idea what it looks like?"

"Yes, it is a small black book, smaller than a wallet. Astin kept addresses and telephone numbers here in France and also in America. I also used it for the same reason that he did up until a few years ago."

Going through several of her business suits, she finally found the small black book and shouted "Yes! Yes! Here Alex, I found it."

Looking through the book they found a page that had five combinations. They returned to Alex's bedroom, trying each combination to open the lock. Disgusted, they tried again and again, none of the combinations worked.

"I guess the best thing we can do is to have a locksmith try to open it."

That afternoon a locksmith arrived to try his expertise on opening the lock, finally admitting that he had given up and refusing money for his efforts. After dinner that evening, Alex looked at the metal case again and noticed some small numbers and letters on three sides of the case. Writing them on a piece of paper they resembled a possible combination. Using a magnifying glass he was able to locate a point to start, turns left or right and numbers to stop. He tried the combination of numbers and letters and was shocked when the case sprung open. He called Claudette to see what he had done and now both were laughing about the incident.

Reading the addresses, notes and letters chronicling Astin's time as a child living north of Savannah, Georgia, with his brothers and sisters, time is as a young boy leaving home to find an education, then as a young man buying a small cotton mill making cloth for the Civil War armies of the North and South, operating a uniform factory in Philadelphia and marrying a daughter of a wealthy senator. It was now three in the morning.

Claudette told Alex, "My vision is blurred from all this reading. It is time to go to bed. We can continue reading on after a good sleep."

Alex agreed going to bed, was the sensible thing to do. Waking at noon, he met Claudette in the kitchen. She looked very tired.

"How do you feel?" he asked.

"I am still very tired, Alex. Maybe we should forget reading papers about Astin's life and just relax today."

A Proposition

Alex and Claudette sat out on the porch discussing moments in their lives when Claudette asked Alex, "What do you intend to do with your life now?"

"Well, I have plenty of money. I would like to visit the places where Astin has been and meet some of his friends and maybe some of my cousins. I would like you, mother, to come with me. I have never seen America and together we could have a good time."

Claudette replied, "Well, there are the leather companies that need my attention and winter is coming on so it would be best if we go next spring. In the meantime, you could help me with the operation of all three leather factories."

Alex was kept busy with the day by day events of his work presented by Claudette who kept his mind off memories of the war and his part in the assassination of the three German generals.

Past Memories

Late one afternoon Alex received a telephone call from Sylvia Mundi which came as a total surprise since he had not heard from her in the past four years. After exchanging greetings, she proposed that they have dinner the following evening at the Cask Cellar Restaurant at five. Alex told Claudette he was going to have dinner with Sylvia Mundi, an acquaintance he knew from his time spent in Casablanca, Morocco.

Claudette with a smile on her face said, "Was she your lover while you were living there? Do not be shy Alex. I am just curious."

"Sylvia is a married woman and we both had a strong relationship during that time. A good understanding and relationship developed."

The following afternoon Alex took a taxi to the Cask Cellar Restaurant and arrived late. His eyes searched the tables for a glimpse of Sylvia.

A maître d' approached him and asked, "May I help you sir?"

"Yes, I am looking for the Mundi table?"

"Follow me sir. It is this way."

Alex followed and immediately noticed Sylvia with a black man and his black child at the table. Sylvia greeted Alex as she rose from her seat to introduce her husband Henri, and their son, Orlin. During the dinner a number of topics were discussed about their respective work and the economy. Orlin needed to go to the restroom so Henri took Orlin by the hand and left. Sylvia immediately told Alex that Orlin was born after their love affair in Casablanca.

"Henri believes he is the proud father of their son and called it a miracle. I know that you can keep this secret that you are the father of my son. I wish in the coming months you would oblige me in a romantic manner. I desire to have a sexual relationship with you so I could have a second child by you. I will make all the arrangements and keep our meetings a treasured secret. Please Alex, please say yes."

"Sylvia, let me think about this before we both get involved in this arrangement."

Moments later, Henri arrived at the table with his son and looking directly into Alex's eyes said, "My son seems to have features that resemble you in a small way. Do not you agree?"

"I do not believe that is true. When children are young, they tend to look like someone else and even when they reach their twenties they do not look like anyone else in their family. Humans are different and there facial differences are also that way. You and your son have dark skin which is caused by either the father or mother passing on their mixed blood to your child. Sylvia's skin is white, the same color white that I am and you are dark skinned like your son. This makes it very easy to determine who in your family passed on mixed blood to your son."

"I understand what you are saying. Thank you for refreshing my mind." was Henri's reply.

Time passed by quickly this evening and before parting they agreed to have dinner again at some later time in the future. Riding home in a taxi Alex kept thinking of the proposition that Sylvia had made and the many questions that were still unanswered.

"How could that young boy born to Sylvia me my son?" he wondered aloud. "Is Sylvia of mixed blood? Does she have another mixed blood lover? Is there maybe more than one other lover? Is it true that she has only had sexual relationships with her husband and me?"

Alex was aware that Sheila had a son who is black. Sheila had mentioned that her father had married a dark-skinned Ethiopian and that she was of mixed blood. That seemed like a reasonable explanation to quell Alex's doubts. He was sure that he was not of mixed blood but the only way to prove that he was not was to marry someone who was white. How could he prove or be sure that there was no connection between black and white in his families past generations.

He will start to search for the truth of his heritage. There were messages to call Sylvia at his office and home. Alex did not return her calls. Claudette left to attend business matters at the two other companies in Casablanca.

Henri had taken his son to see his mother in Egypt and would be gone for two weeks. This gave Sylvia a perfect opportunity to entice Alex into a lovemaking affair. It was Friday night and they would have the weekend together. Alex entered his waiting taxi and was surprised to find Sylvia sitting there smiling and saying,

"I hope you do not mind I have already given the taxi driver directions on where we are going."

"Where are we going?" Alex questioned.

"You will see Alex. Soon, you will see."

They finally arrived at the Château Mont Blanc and went to the reservation desk were Sylvia told the clerk they had a reservation under the name of Mr. and Mrs. Bolan. Sylvia registered and printed her first name as Jean and Alex was Bill Bolan. Alex needed the location of a pay phone and was directed to one in the lobby. He called home. Cook answered the telephone and Alex told a fictitious story that he had met some old friends and was staying at their home and would not be back until the following week.

Together he and Sylvia had a fine dinner with a delicious burgundy wine. Alex still felt uneasy about what he was going to do at Sylvia's insistence. The room at this hotel was quite unique. It had a large circular pool that had been cut out from the white marble stone to a four foot depth and was filled by a small stream of water which came from the hot springs outside the hotel. Alex looked at the thermometer which recorded the water temperature of hundred degrees Fahrenheit. Sylvia sat down next to Alex holding a bowl containing crushed lotus blossoms in a light yellow sauce.

Alex looked at Sylvia, "What is this?"

"Anyone who drinks this potion will enjoy sexual desire beyond his imagination and dreams."

"Sylvia, where did you learn to make this potion?"

"Henri brought it from Egypt and told me that it had been handed down through the ages by the Kings of the pyramids. It was used by men and women to have long sexual activities, sometimes lasting many hours. Henri and I tried used this potion many times in a hope that I would become pregnant but it never happened. Our lovemaking in Casablanca proved to me that I was a fertile woman. Yes, Alex, you are the one who gave me a meaning to life."

They both slowly sipped the potion with their wine which led to emotional expressions at the edge of the pool where they both hurriedly undressed and stepped into the warm water, enjoying the desires of one another. Hours passed, as they continued loving one another in many different ways. Alex could not believe how aggressive he was with Sylvia, who was urging him on. The light of dawn appeared, and they decided to take a restful sleep.

Sylvia kissed Alex, which made him open his eyes and asked him if he would like to have dinner in their room? He agreed and they both took a quick shower and wrapped themselves in their warm terrycloth bathrobes. Dinner arrived a short time later and on the table lying in a small bowl of water were four lotus blossom flowers. Alex jokingly said to Sylvia, "I think we should eat the lotus blossoms first and forget the dinner."

"I think we'd better eat first, otherwise we will both die from loss of strength and exhaustion!" was her response.

The dinner finished, Sylvia crushed two lotus blossom flowers and added a black sauce.

"What is this black sauce made from?" Alex asked.

Sylvia replied. It is made from Anisette, a black seed that encourages sexual desire."

They decided to disrobe and step into the pool while sipping their exotic potion when once again Alex fell into the grip of Sylvia's aggressive foreplay becoming aroused by her actions. They decided to continue their desires for one another in the bedroom. They spent hours satisfying each other until a restful sleep had overtaken them.

Alex was awakened by Sylvia's playful loving which prompted Alex to become loving and aroused in his enjoyment with her. With no breakfast or lunch, they decided to have an excellent dinner after which Sylvia crushed the lotus blossoms and Anisette They slowly consumed the potion while enjoying foreplay in the pool. A short time later he was aroused again as Sylvia continued her aggressive foreplay. Alex could not believe his continued strength and desire for making love. He was experiencing the most exhilarating time of his life. Never before had he felt so free to give his love and receive more from Sylvia. He was delirious and did not want to stop his seductive movements and long-lasting control.

Glorious Ending

Sylvia finally got Alex's attention, while still in a compromising position, and told him that the hotel bill had been paid. Also she told him that at five am on the following day she would leave for the station and would board a train for Paris at five thirty. He was to leave on the next train at six thirty. They should not be seen leaving the hotel together or returning on the same train to Paris.

"I will go home, change clothing and be at work at nine. You, Alex, should go home and do the same. I have arranged to have two taxis waiting for our departure to the trains."

Alex wanted to have Sylvia come to bed and enjoy their last moments of lovemaking. Sylvia told Alex that she had a wonderful time and enjoyed his aggressive lovemaking.

A knock sounded on the door at four thirty in the morning and Sylvia and Alex both washed and dressed. Another knock led Alex to open the door to see a waiter with a tray of pastry and coffee wheeled in on a small table near the warm pool. They both sat down and enjoyed the light breakfast smiling at one another but hardly saying a word.

Finally Sylvia said, "I have to go." She gave Alex a long-lasting kiss and said, "I am going to miss you. I hope that somewhere or somehow we can meet and enjoy one another again."

Alex left a sizable tip for the waiter then left for the waiting taxi which arrived at its train station moments before he was to leave for Paris. He purchased his ticket and had an uneventful ride by train and taxi to his house. Entering the kitchen, the cook and maid were glad to see him.

The cook asked Alex, "Did you have a good time with your friends?"

"Yes, I had a very good time. Now, what for breakfast? Do I smell sausages with French toast and coffee? Any calls from my mother?"

"No, we have not had any telephone calls from anyone."

Alex finished breakfast, went to the bedroom, undressed and took a warm shower and soon was on his way to work. Business was very good and the days went by quickly. By the end of the second week, a phone call from Claudette informed Alex that her work was finished in Casablanca and she would be coming home by a new means of travel.

"Alex, I am so excited to be flying home, in an airplane!"

She hoped that he would meet her at the airport and would call him later to tell him what her time of arrival at the airport would be. Alex continued with his duties in the operation of the leather company and never realized that he was working twelve to fourteen hours each day. He called cook with a reminder that he would be late for dinner and to place food in the warming oven which he would have when he arrived home.

Claudette called the following Saturday, from the airport and told Alex she would be leaving from Casablanca at eleven in the morning with arrival at the Paris airport scheduled at four in the afternoon. Alex wished her good luck and reassured her he that he would not be late. He arrived at the airport at three-thirty. The weather was cold and rainy but he had a good view of the landing area. He purchased a newspaper, and while starting to read the events of the past day he felt a tap on its shoulder.

Looking up he was surprised to see Lee Bisset standing there smiling and asking, "What brings you here on this rainy day?"

Alex explained that he was waiting for Claudette, who was flying in from Casablanca. Lee told Alex that he never called her back about having dinner and an evening together. Alex explained the business was keeping him very busy, twelve to sometimes fourteen hours a day, which left little time for dinner or an evening out.

"Working all those hours, leaves me tired and probably a bore to be with."

"Alex, if time permits, I would like to show you my factory that produces a variety of items from leather." She left her calling card that had two telephone numbers, saying, "Call me. I am really serious about finding out what you are like, dressed or undressed."

Confusing Papers

Claudette's plane arrived in a rainy downpour and she hurried into the lobby greeting Alex with a fresh smile on her face.

"Flying above the clouds and seeing so much of the world from the window of the plane was the most wonderful experience I ever had. You really must try flying, you will enjoy it. Here take my luggage. Now let us find a taxi for our ride home."

The rain had stopped as the taxi pulled up to the curb of the home. The cook and maid were standing at the front door. Claudette gave them both a generous hug then telling them she was hungry for the cook's food. After dinner, Claudette and Alex discussed the operation of the three leather companies until ten that evening when it was decided that more could be accomplished after a good night's sleep and a refreshed mind.

The following morning after breakfast, Claudette asked Alex, "Have you read any of the papers from Astin's locked case?"

"No, I thought it would be best if you and I looked at them together."

"Thank you for being considerate."

They opened the steel case and started reading some of Astin's notes on where he lived and what he did in his life and America and the people he knew. The money he accumulated was apparently still in the Union Bank of Philadelphia as was a paper mill in Valley Forge, from the Civil War of 1863. It all was too much to digest.

Claudette suggested that Alex try to put all of Astin's travels in a chronological sequence so that they would be able to know where he was at different times in his life. Alex began to align the papers and notes according to their dates and soon found that it had already been done by Astin. As he filed the papers in the middle space of the metal case he started to read the notes. They began with Astin as a young boy on a farm in Georgia

Claudette at end of the room asked Alex, "Are you having any success?"

"Everything is in perfect order. Astin had filed everything by dates, names and addresses which can be followed easily. We can go through all them being sure that we do not mix the dates out of their proper order."

After a full day of reading Astin's notes and letters they decided to retrace his life in America. They agreed that the best time to travel would be in mid-April by ship from Amsterdam to Savannah, Georgia. Money for their travel would be converted from francs to American currency. They also decided that before they left they would give every employee in the three leather companies a twenty-five percent ownership in their businesses. This would all be done in a legal manner, registering the documents with the courts during the month of February. Claudette decided to fly once again to Casablanca and inform the employees of their new ownership in the Luster and LeaBeau leather companies and she planned to return the following week.

Alex spent time with lawyers who were drawing up the documents for the employees, when stepping out of the court building he saw Lee Bisset and greeted her with a pleasant smile. During the conversation she suggested that they have dinner at the Rouge Restaurant at six this evening and then enjoy each other for a night out and maybe more if he was up to it. Alex agreed and would meet her at the restaurant.

Later that afternoon, Alex took a taxi to the Egyptian section of Paris where he found a small shop dealing in exotic and medicinal drugs. He asked the clerk if he had any lotus blossoms and Anisette. The clerk became very excited and nervous telling Alex that Anisette was a powerful drug used to heighten the sexual desires in men and women and was illegal in France. He asked Alex if he was a government drug enforcer. Alex responded that he had used it in the past and needed enough for two evenings. The clerk took him in the back room and promptly put the lotus blossoms with the Anisette into a small decorated tea box. The clerk told Alex to tell no one about what the box contained. He hurriedly paid for his goods and walked for a short distance to a taxi, which drove him home. After a quick shower and change of clothing he placed the tea box into his coat pocket and arrived at the restaurant a few minutes late.

Lee remarked, "I was beginning to think that you would back out of this commitment. Come sit down have some wine. I have ordered dinner to be served at six-thirty. I do not like eating late. It's just a routine that I follow. I like being in control, it makes me feel secure."

During dinner, Lee said to Alex, "I would like you to see one of my shops that process your hides into an assortment of items for people in all walks of life."

Alex agreed to take a tour as soon as they finished dinner. They took a short taxi ride to her shop which had a large display of finished leather goods in the window, a room in the rear for processing and designing different types of patterns on the leather. Alex was really impressed, telling Lee he had no idea that finished leather could be so appealing. Leaving her store she suggested to Alex that they share a bottle of wine at her home. Alex agreed and touched his side pocket to make sure that the box was still there. She instructed the cab driver in detailed steps of how he would arrive at her home and during the ten mile drive she was constantly advising him with directions until they arrived at her home, which was a short distance from the Seine River.

She told Alex there was a bottle of wine in the kitchen and would he please open it while she changed into some comfortable clothing. Alex looking for the wine noticed a tea box similar to the one in his pocket which he removed and compared. Yes, they were identical in all aspects including the same type of box. He opened her tea box and found it contained lotus blossoms with a packet of Anisette seeds. He quickly put the cover back on the tea box and said to himself, "Two minds with a single thought."

Lee said to Alex, "You have not opened the wine."

Alex used an excuse, saying, "I could not find the cork puller."

Lee handed him the puller which was lying next to the wine bottle. Not saying another word, he opened the bottle of wine and poured two glasses while sitting in the living room. After consuming several glasses of wine from the bottle, Alex told Lee he should be going home to which she responded with an invitation for him to spend the evening at her house. She went into the kitchen and a short time later came out with two sipping cups, each containing crushed lotus blossom with an Anisette black seed sauce.

"Try this Alex, the Egyptians drank this to enjoy the ecstasy of life and the pleasures it brings."

Alex took a small sip and remarked to Lee that it had a very pleasant taste. A short time later, Lee moved very close to Alex, asking him if he would like more of the Egyptian sauce. Not planning to tell her that he was familiar with this Egyptian love potion he answered by saying, "It had aroused his desire to make passionate love to her."

Lee replied, "Not yet Alex. I want you to be fully relaxed and very passionate. Go into my bathroom and change into one of my long bathrobes that you will find in the closet next to the door."

Everything was where Lee said it would be. Alex hurriedly undressed and put the longest bathrobe on with the bottom touching the floor. He then hurried into the living room where Lee was entering with two more cups of you are Egyptian love potion. This they continued to sip during their foreplay which became more aggressive. Lee opened her robe, which exposed her beautiful body causing Alex to draw her to him in a firm embrace and began kissing her repeatedly. She opened Alex's robe and the two warm bodies melted into one.

Alex wanted more of Lee to which she responded by saying, "Not here Alex not here. Come to the bedroom. We will share our delight, together for the rest of the night."

Alex found Lee's erotic motions and positions different from anything he had ever experienced before and so went the evening. With the coming of dawn, still entwined in each other's arms, it felt as if neither one would let go. It was midday, when Alex was awakened to the clatter of dishes in the kitchen. There he saw Lee, making breakfast for them.

After going to the bathroom Alex walked into the kitchen and gave Lee a warm loving kiss, to which she responded by saying, "I never thought that you could express your feelings to me in the way you just did. That was a surprise that I will never forget."

As they ate breakfast, Lee remarked, "It is too bad that I do not have any more of that Egyptian potion. It would be wonderful to have more of what we had yesterday and this morning."

"Lee, I too would love to enjoy those moments again today."

They finished their breakfast upon which time Alex removed the tea box from his coat pocket and handed it to Lee.

Looking at it she said, "It was empty and that there was nothing left."

"Open it," Alex replied.

"Why do you want me to do that, I told you the box is empty." She reluctantly opened it seeing the lotus blossoms with a packet of Anisette seeds. Turning to Alex, "Are you sure you want to do this?"

His reply was "Yes, again and again."

He was amazed that Lee could become so open to carrying on conversations on a number of subjects along with a very deep satisfying love to hold Alex's continued interest.

A Journey of Surprises

It was late Sunday evening when Alex told Lee that it was time for him to return home. He needed to rest up and work in the coming weeks on the preparations for his trip to America with his mother Claudette. He held and kissed Lee, while she whispered. "I never felt like this before."

"I think I am falling in love with you Alex. It is a nice feeling, and I will miss you. While you are in America I will be in different parts of Europe and Asia. Goodbye for now, Alex my sweet."

Leaving by taxi he arrived home at eleven and went straight to his bedroom to change into his night clothing and was soon asleep under his warm, featherbed comforter. The following three weeks were filled with the pressures of business and trip preparations including obtaining passports and getting passenger reservations from Antwerp to Savannah, Georgia. They would be leaving on April first at ten in the morning. Claudette was still in Casablanca and in a telephone conversation with Alex she told him that she would fly out from Casablanca on the twenty-first of March and also that the transfer of the twenty-five percent share of the two companies had been completed. Alex had made the same announcement to the employees at the LeaBeau leather company in Paris. The employees were overwhelmed with gratitude and promises of making the company even more profitable.

Alex lost track of the days and realized that Claudette would be leaving Casablanca in a few days. He hurried through his obligations and finally all preparations for the trip were completed. Claudette arrived at the airport on twenty first of March. They decided to each pack one small suitcase. Alex would put Astin's metal case in his luggage for safe keeping. By train, they left for Antwerp on March thirtieth, staying overnight in a hotel a short distance from the dock. The following day, Alex confirmed their passage on a German ship called the Viscount which was a fast-moving freighter with a passenger upper deck. It was large enough to accommodate two hundred people in suitable staterooms. Boarding and assignment of staterooms started at promptly at eight on morning of April first. Alex and Claudette had adjoining rooms with a privacy door between them. Promptly at ten in the evening the ship moved out into the open channel with the help of two tugboats, which pointed the Viscount into the open sea.

"It seems for a freighter that we were going extremely fast" said Alex told Claudette.

"How long will the cruise take?"

Alex speaking in German asked a seaman, "Do you know how many days it will take to reach Savannah, Georgia?"

"Six or seven days sir, depending on the weather."

The accommodations were good and the flavor of the German food brought back memories for Alex of the time he spent in Germany. The seas were calm and the days were sunny. Sailing was smooth, with the bow of the boat slicing through the water like a sharp knife through a piece of meat. On the afternoon of the fifth day the loudspeaker broke the silence by announcing that the ship would be in the port of Savannah by seven the next morning and breakfast would be served at six. Claudette was happy that they had arrived at Savannah and was really looking forward to traveling in America. They had a hearty breakfast, then taking their luggage; they walked down the gangplank to the dock.

Claudette turned to Alex and said, "I have never seen so many black people. I wonder if America is mostly black people."

"What is this white material?" Alex asked, pointing to some bales stacked on the dock.

The man replied. "It's cotton that's being shipped to Germany where it will be processed and woven into different types of cloth." He then pulled a handful of cotton from the bale and handed it to Alex who thanked him for the cotton ball.

By noon, the temperature and humidity had risen to a point where it was very uncomfortable. They asked the taxi driver to take them to a hotel with eating facilities. It was not too long before they arrived at a beautiful mansion that had been converted into a hotel and dining room.

"Everyone is black," Claudette whispered to Alex. "Are you sure were in the right place? I have not seen a white person since we came here, they are nice and polite, but I do not want to stay in a black hotel."

No sooner had she finished saying that when a white gentleman approached them.

"Hello, I am Mr. Jefferson, the owner of this establishment."

He showed them beautiful rooms with ten foot high ceilings and fans turning in a slow manner. Dinner was served from five to seven in the evening and breakfast was served seven to nine. They all walked about the garden area.

"Mr. Jefferson, do you know the location of a small town ten miles to the north called Spliton."

"Yes, it's a group of about 15 houses; you can't miss it. During the slave trade it was quite prosperous and had a notorious sheriff that enjoyed killing blacks. There was a group of Southerners who were eventually punished and put into jail where most of them died. They say it was the peanut growing capital of America. You will need an automobile to get there. A man by the name of Pierce has a big garage that repairs automobiles and sometimes has good used cars cheap."

Alex left Claudette at the hotel while he went to talk to Pierce about purchasing a used car. He looked at several cars and decided on the closed-in touring model. It carried two spare tires in the front and two in the back with a small rack in the rear to hold a ten gallon gasoline can. The price was six hundred and twenty-five dollars. Alex took the car for a test drive and returned to the garage a short time later agreeing to pay the price for the car. Leaving that transaction behind, he rode back to the hotel telling Claudette what he had done to make the trip easier.

She replied by saying, "This is going to be an experience similar to flying from Casablanca."

The night at the hotel was hot and very humid. Sleep was almost impossible until the early morning hours when there was finally enough cool air. By ten that morning they started their trip to Spliton. The road being bumpy and rutted by farm wagons made for slow going. As they approached their destination, they noticed a weathered sign, which read, "Capital of the Finest Peanuts", "Grown by the, VanEpp family in 1836."

Alex handed Claudette a short letter written by Astin to his sister, Freda stating that he was now thirteen years old and very homesick. Driving up the road, they saw the remainder of Astin's home and that of Freda's, who lived a short distance on across the road. Leaving that memory behind, they stopped at the cluster of empty, rundown homes. A young black man walked up to the car and asked Alex if he was lost. Alex stated that that they were looking for some distant relatives by the name of VanEpp. He replied that the best way to get that information was to go to the county assessor's office. He gave them directions on how to get to the city of Greystone which was fifteen miles to the north.

They continued driving on that road but it was almost impassable. Finally, after two hours they arrived in Greystone, a pleasant, clean looking town where they found rooms for the night and enjoyed a delicious chicken dinner. The following morning after getting directions on how to get to the assessor's office, they left their hotel. It was a short walk from the hotel. They entered the office where they were politely greeted by a young woman.

"What can I assist you in finding? What is your interest?"

Alex replied, "We are looking for relatives on my father's side of the family."

"The name?" she asked.

"VanEpp," Alex replied.

She brought out a large book and began thumbing through the pages. She located ninety-one individuals with the same last name, all living in a small village called Weatherford, twenty-two miles west of Greystone. Alex thanked her for the information and left with Claudette now heading for Greystone on a very good road.

As they entered the town they saw American flags and large red, white and blue banners hanging from every building on the main road. Stopping in front of the bank an elderly black man with American ribbons hanging from his suit coat approached Alex and wanted to know why he and Claudette were there. Alex responded by saying he was looking for relatives with the VanEpp name.

A crowd gathered around Alex and Claudette yelling. "We are all VanEpps. Today is our holiday. We are now a town with a new name registered as Epptown."

Alex was surprised to hear what they were saying and told the crowd of blacks that they were VanEpps and looking for relatives. One of the older men invited them into his house offering them lemonade. He told them that the VanEpp children had left home to work as sharecroppers. One of the brothers, Astin, returned years later and gave each of his brothers and sisters a large amount of money so they could own their homes and buy land.

"Then he left and we never heard from him again."

"Is there any other information? Do you know if there are any immediate relatives surviving?"

"Astin was born a white boy, the youngest in the family but I am sure he was black under his skin. We have all done well and prospered after the Civil War. We have taken care of our own and not allowed whites to trash in our town. We have one old man who claims to be the surviving son of the VanEpp family. They did peanut farming north of Savannah a long time ago. I will take you over there and you can have a talk with him. He might know something about your father."

It was midday, when they arrived at the old man's house. They introduced themselves as a wife and son of Astin.

Alex was first to ask the question, "Did you know, my father?"

The old man replied, "Yes, I knew him very well. He was last child in our family born white and one year younger than me. My father, Ayer, had no way of sending any of us go to school because we are black and Astin could not go to school because he lived with a black family. When Astin was twelve years old my father had him leave the family and hoped that he could find schooling up north. He was born white and when he returned sometime later he continued to look white. He gave all of us money for homes and land after the Civil War and this town was built from money given to us by Astin. That is why the town is now called Epptown."

After all hours of talking and reminiscing the old man finally said "My name is Ned, the fourth child in the VanEpp family. My brothers and sisters have passed away some time ago. My day will come when the Lord thinks I have had enough time here on earth."

Thanking Ned, for all his information. Claudette and Alex took a slow walk back to the local hotel discussing what Ned had said and surprised to learn that Astin was born into a black family, Claudette could not believe what she had heard and was convinced that most of the talk about Astin was a fabrication of Ned's old mind. She needed more proof and was willing and hopeful to search for it.

It was now the end of April. The townspeople were busy with planting cotton and a variety of crops. Claudette and Alex decided it was time to leave and drive to Charleston where Astin had lived for a few years. The trip was slow, wet and muddy and on two different occasions Alex had to get the services of a farmer with a team of horses to pull the car out of the mire. After eight days of travel they arrived in Charleston. Still not convinced that Astin was of mixed blood, Alex felt it was impossible for him to accept the notion that it meant that he was also of mixed blood. From the street address in one of Astin's letters they found their way to a pile of rubble containing some machinery and bricks strewn about the surrounding area.

Claudette remarked, "Maybe that is where the cotton mill used to be. Do you think, so, Alex?"

"You may be right."

With a excited voice, Claudette shouted! "Look over there. Alex, I see a part of a building through the brush and trees. It may be a house."

Together they walked toward the building only to find it was badly burned except for the steps and a patio which were made of cement and stone.

"Well, there is nothing left for us to do. There are no houses or people in the area to talk to. I suggest that we find a hotel for the night and try to get directions on how to get to Philadelphia."

Driving into the city they found a mansion that had been converted into a hotel, completely renovated with pleasant rooms and a dining room next to the kitchen. A young black boy placed their luggage in two adjoining rooms. They had a glass of wine before sitting down to a dinner of ham, potatoes, and black-eyed peas. Dessert was a large piece of apple pie with a small dish of tart lemon meringue, which was something they had never tasted before and found it to be very good. Totally relaxed after their meal, they decided to go to their rooms and sleep with no time set for rising in the morning.

At ten o'clock Claudette knocked on Alex's door and said, "It is time to get up. I will meet you in the dining room for breakfast."

Alex, barely awake, stumbled into the bathroom taking a long, warm shower, dressed and met Claudette in the dining room. The menu did not have any options or choices; it was two eggs, bacon, bread, pancakes and grits.

Alex asked the waitress, "What are grits?"

She replied. "Its white corn that has been boiled into a porridge."

They had their breakfast with coffee and both of them sampled the grits to which they both agreed it had a pleasant taste.

A young lady came over to their table,, "Did you enjoy your breakfast?"

"Yes, I was very good. There were foods we have not had before."

"Thank you. Was there anything else you might need?"

Alex responded immediately, "Yes, we want to know what is the best route to Philadelphia, Pennsylvania and where can I get my car serviced before we leave?"

"I will take care of giving you a map and service of your car. I need the keys to your car, please."

Alex reached into his coat pocket and pulled out his key's, which she took.

"I will drop off your car and should be back in about twenty minutes with a travel map of roads leading to Philadelphia."

She returned a short time later, telling them that their car would be back in less than two hours. Handing Alex the map, she pointed out that she had outlined a number of roads with red pencil for travel on their trip.

"Thank you. Also, if there was no problem we will stay another night and leave after breakfast in the morning."

Rising early, they had their usual breakfast with Alex, avoiding the grits on his plate, telling Claudette in confidence that he did not like the taste. Alex paid their bill for breakfast, lodging and service to the car. With their luggage in the car, they decided to drive on the road along the seashore to enjoy the sunny day and the smell of the open sea.

For several days they rode stopping at small hotels at night and enjoying fresh seafood during the day. Arriving at the outskirts of Philadelphia, they asked a hotel manager for directions on how to get to the Union Bank. He gave them a printed map showing the streets and interesting landmarks in the city. They were to follow a blue crayon line that he had outlined to the Union Bank. One hour later they arrived at their destination. Since it was midday they decided to stop at the Union Bank and settle their business before lunch. They entered the bank, showing their credentials to a clerk who hurriedly went to the bank president's office. Moments later, the bank president introduced himself and invited them into his office where two elderly black men rose from their chairs and were introduced.

"This is John Christon, a Vice President dealing in legal matters, and this is Christopher Christon, Vice President of Accounting."

They all sat down at a long table with several documents that had been signed by Astin. The 1880 financial statement was presented by Christopher, who indicated the total worth of Astin's investments totaled six million, eight hundred and fifty thousand. The Valley Forge paper mill, which had no debt, had on deposit three million and forty seven thousand with an assessed value of slightly over four million. All city, state and federal taxes were paid. Claudette and Alex were dumbfounded by what they had heard. The bank president informed them that any changes could be accomplished by contacting John Christon.

It was nearing five in the afternoon so Alex invited the bank president, John and Christopher to dinner. The bank president had made other commitments and could not join him at dinner. John and Christopher took Alex and Claudette to a restaurant that carried a variety of different foods. Once seated, John ordered a French Burgundy wine that brought back memories of France for Alex and Claudette. Dinner was excellent and much more than one could eat.

John started his story. "There is something you must know about Astin. He was married to our mother, Sally who gave birth to a black child- me. I was brought to St. Joan Catholic orphanage where I remained under the teachings of the nuns through my adolescent and college years. Christopher arrived three years later and went through the same schooling as I did. It was not until I was twenty-three that I was told I had a brother in the same orphanage. When Christopher graduated from college we were told that we had separate accounts in the Union Bank left there by Astin. Presenting our account numbers at the bank, we were informed that each had an account totaling more than one hundred and twenty-five thousand. We asked who the donor of this money was. The bank replied it was a private matter and the name could never be given to anyone. While sitting in a restaurant across the street, a young man dropped a note on our table then hurried through the kitchen. We never saw him again. We did not even know what he looked like. The note read, the donor to your account is Astin VanEpp. His address is in the Villa Sixteen of the French Riviera."

Alex and Claudette became very excited and could hardly control themselves from not speaking.

John went on with the rest of the story. "Christopher and I decided to meet Astin. We saw him while you, Claudette, were away on business in Paris. We talked for some time. Astin asked only one question. Do you want to change your last name to VanEpp? No, we decided a long time ago, to keep the names given to us by the nuns. It was a pleasant visit and it was nice to know who are father really was. Here are copies of our birth certificates given to us when we were twenty-three years old and when we had decided to leave St. Joan Catholic seminary. As you can see it indicates our dates of birth and our mother and father's names. So, Alex, like it or not, we are brothers of mixed blood."

Claudette was speechless while Alex was having a terrible time trying to digest all the information that John had just related. The waiter came over to the table and told him that the restaurant was closing for the night.

Before leaving Alex turned to John and Christopher, "If there is ever anything you need now or in the future, here is our address in Paris."

Christopher smiled and said, "I already have your address in your private accounting ledger."

Alex asked, "Why did you wait so long to tell us this?"

Looking at Christopher, John replied, "We decided it would be best if we met together rather than writing to you and Claudette about this matter, which would sound unbelievable, and possibly not true at all."

They finished the evening by agreeing to stay in contact with one another. Claudette and Alex went to their adjacent hotel rooms Claudette came into Alex's bedroom totally upset about learning that Astin had kept his families' mixed marriage a secret.

"Would you have married him if you had known his family's history?" Alex remarked, "What happened is done. There is no way to reverse what happened in the past except to be aware of its existence in the future at which time a sound decision, well thought out, can be made."

They enjoyed the next two weeks, visiting the points of interest and historic monuments in Philadelphia.

Alex asked, Claudette. "Do you want to continue on to Santa Fe New Mexico, and California?"

"Yes. Knowing the places of the rest of Astin's travels is important to me."

The automobile had been serviced and four new tires installed for the trip to Santa Fe. The countryside was beautiful and the trip across the Great Plains showed the land covered with corn and golden fields of wheat, oats and barley for miles and miles. It abruptly stopped in New Mexico with Santa Fe fifty miles to the north. They inquired at a gas station after eight days of travel for directions to the governor's home. The attendant pointed to a road across the highway and said it was twenty-five miles up that road and you certainly cannot miss it as the size of the house was big, very big.

They arrived at the governor's home and were immediately stopped by a security guard who asked them for what reason had they come here?

Alex explained, "My father had this very home constructed for his wife, Sally, who passed away and was buried somewhere in this area. He then sold it to the governor with some land, giving the remaining land to the Indians that lived in the area."

The guard said he knew where Sally was buried and said, "It is a short walk. Come with me."

They walked up to a large iron fence that surrounded one tombstone with the epithet roughly chiseled out of the stone.

"Here lies Sally, beloved wife of Astin.

Only now, the pain of life follows her no more."

Claudette told Alex that Astin had lost his wife to sickness.

"It is a beautiful spot and I am sure Astin spent many hours by her grave."

They decided to leave this beautiful area and travel on to California. Alex was tiring of the long trips and Claudette had to nudge him quite often when he was starting to travel off the road. It was now August, very hot and dry through Arizona with San Diego still three full days of driving ahead. When at last they arrived in San Diego, Alex was completely exhausted and dehydrated. They found a hotel not too far from the dock where Alex spent the next day trying to recuperate from his ordeal of driving. Claudette did some shopping and purchased plenty of liquids and food. After recuperating most of the week, Claudette and Alex started looking in the telephone directory. And yes, there was one VanEpp.

He copied the name and telephone number on a piece of paper and said to Claudette, "This must be Astin's daughter. I am sure it is. Look how it is spelled in the directory, Astina."

Alex became very excited and hurried to the telephone to call Astina. The phone started ringing with Alex urging someone to answer his call. After several rings, Alex was starting to give up the call when a voice responded to his call, "Hello, this is Astina. Who is calling, please?"

"Hello. My name is Alex VanEpp and I think we could be related. Would you have the time for me and my mother to discuss our lineage?"

"Yes. Where would you like to meet? My apartment would be best, it is quiet and private. You have my address and my apartment number is two, located on the first floor. If you have no pressing appointments, then I suggest one-thirty this afternoon.

"We are looking forward to meeting you."

Alex told Claudette, what had transpired in the telephone conversation with Astina and that they were going to meet her at this afternoon. Claudette suggested that they have an early lunch before going to see Astina.

A Final Link

They had an early lunch and decided to take a taxi to Astina's. Arriving on time, Claudette and Astin looked at the bronze plaque which in large bold letters read VanEpp Apartments. A knock on the door of number two revealed to Alex's eyes a tall, dark haired woman with Asian features and a beautiful, captivating smile. With her soft voice she could control anyone in her presence.

After all the introductions were made, they sat down in a beautifully furnished Oriental parlor. She told them of her grandmother's love affair with her grandfather, a ship captain traveling throughout the Far East.

"My grandmother, Kina passed away when my mother, Maleta, was three years old. I was raised by my grandfather when my mother passed away later."

"Maleta had just finished college at the age of twenty-two. A year later, she was introduced to Astin by a college friend and their romance continued for quite some time, even after I was born and given the name Astina. He told my mother that he would be leaving to see his parents somewhere around Savannah, Georgia. He left and never returned. My mother was heartbroken, and always made up excuses of how he must have died. She waited day after day hoping for a letter or news of his whereabouts."

Astina handed Alex, a picture of Maleta and Astin, together.

"They were a beautiful couple, don't you agree?"

"Yes, they are a fine looking couple but I do not recognize your mother or the man you call Astin." was Alex's reply.

Astina rose from her chair and waited while Claudette looked at the picture agreeing that they were a beautiful couple as she handed the picture back to Astina.

"I will make some coffee or tea, which would you prefer?"

"Tea, if you please, Thank you." Claudette turned to Alex, saying, "Why did you deny that you did not know Astin?"

"By saying that you had put me into the position of denying that I also did not know Astin."

Alex said, "I did not want to blemish her thoughts of Astin. I need more time to think about how we will present this to her."

In a short time, Astina appeared with a pot of tea and an assortment of wafers. They sat and talked about several topics during which Astina asked if we had found any one else with a last name like VanEpp?

Alex quickly replied that "They only knew of relatives that lived in Holland and had not met anyone in America that had this same last name."

Claudette decided it was time to leave and they planned to meet once again and have dinner together. They thanked her for all the information she gave regarding her mother and Astin. They left her apartment, and hailed a taxi during which time not a word was spoken between Claudette and Alex. At the hotel and during dinner, no conversations were started.

In the hotel that evening Claudette walked into Alex's room and in a loud furious voice said, "I am ashamed of how you lied to Astina and how you could be so degrading to yourself and me. It is something that you will have to correct while I am at your side and I hope she forgives us! Tomorrow morning you will telephone her and ask her to have dinner with us tomorrow evening. Is that clear, Alex?"

"Yes mother, I will call her in the morning." It was the first time that Alex had ever seen Claudette in such a rage. He did not realize until now that she had a temper that would make anyone cringe. The following morning he called Astina who agreed to an early dinner at four in the Seabreeze Restaurant, considered to be the best place to eat a variety of seafood. Telling Claudette, where there were going to eat, and the time they were to meet Astina, Claudette nodded her head in approval.

Alex added a jest to Claudette telling her, "It was not a restaurant that serves steaks so there will be no sharp knives!"

There was no response from Claudette and Alex avoided trying to humor her anymore.

That afternoon they took a taxi to the Seabreeze Restaurant and found Astina sitting at a table on the open deck, smiling as they approached her. Alex ordered a white wine for dinner and orders from the menu were given to the waiter. Alex raised his wine glass and proposed a toast that a new lasting friendship had been found. All agreed to that toast. The dinner of seafood was excellent with enough food for everyone.

Alex turned to Astina and said, "I did a terrible thing when talking with you yesterday and my mother and I want you to hear the true story of Astin. My grandfather worked on a slave ship where he took a dark- skinned slave woman for a wife. After leaving the slave ship in Savannah, Georgia, they bought a farm and grew peanuts, which gave them a comfortable profit. Phia gave birth to four dark skinned children. A fifth child was born white. That was Astin. My great grandfather made him leave the farm when he was twelve years old and told him to seek an education elsewhere. He was very intelligent and graduated from a private school, amassing large amounts of money during the Civil War. He married a socialite, Sally, who was the daughter of a highly respected senator. Their first child was a black. This so troubled her, she became addicted to alcohol. When the second child was born black, she continued to drink heavily and died in Santa Fe, New Mexico. He left and met your mother here in San Diego and during the time they were together you, Astina, were born. Astin left to visit his family in Georgia, where his father was very sick and wanted to return to his farm in Holland. On a ship leaving New York for Amsterdam he met my mother, Claudette, and they married a year later. I am their child."

Alex looked over at Claudette and noticed she was crying and Astina was crying as she rose from her chair. Walking over to Astin, hugging and kissing him than saying, "We are of mixed blood. We are brother and sister and you Claudette will always be my aunt."

Astina told them that she was financially secure because of what Astin did for her mother. "My only regret was that I never found a person such as you, Alex, to fall in love with and marry."

"What lies ride in a person's mind can only be sequestered by the truth." That was the final toast given by Claudette.

They welcomed Astina to come and visit them in Paris had hoped it would be soon. They parted with hugs and kisses while waving goodbye to Astina. On the way to the hotel Claudette told Alex that she had made reservations for a Pullman car on a transcontinental train from San Diego to New York City, which they were to board in two days.

Alex looked surprised, only saying, "How long will it take to arrive in New York City?"

"It will take six days, with several stops along the way."

Claudette called the following day to confirm their reservations and found everything was in order for their coast-to-coast trip. With a boarding time of eleven in the morning, Alex said, "What are we going to do with our automobile?"

Claudette said, "That is quite simple. Just sign it over to Astina and let that be a surprise for her after we leave."

Alex sat down and wrote a short note to Astina about the gift of the automobile and the transfer of ownership to her. He placed the transfer papers and a note in a folder addressed to Astina. He told the desk clerk that he wanted someone to drive the car to her address and give her the folder. There was hundred dollar bill for the person that would perform this obligation. The clerk said he would take care of delivering the car and packet by himself on the following day.

The Long Trip Home

They packed what few pieces of luggage they had and were at the train station shortly after ten. The porter guided them to one of the small Pullman sleeper cars, which was the last one of the cars on the line.

Alex asked the porter, "Why are we in the last car of the line?"

The porter responded, "The last car is reserved for people who don't have to put up with the annoyance of others passing by on their way to the dining tables only two cars away. You have the right to view the country side at the end platform of your car."

Alex thanked him for his explanation, rewarding him with a few silver dollars. The train left the station on time; leaving California behind them and only open spaces with no buildings in view. It was mid-August and the air was as hot and dry as the soot from the steam engine making it uncomfortable to sit out on the platform. Claudette and Alex discussed where they had been and what they had seen and what they had heard many times during the ride to the east. Claudette would repeat over and over that she never thought that Astin was born from mixed blood and he never told her about his life in America. She never suspected that during his life he was involved in affairs with women, leaving a trail of unrest to children and women that he encountered.

Alex asked Claudette, "If what you were told by Astin when you first met that he was of mixed blood would you have broken off your relationship with him?"

"I do not know. When you are in love with many obstacles in your way and if the love is strong enough, those obstacles are ignored."

Alex said, "I am of mixed blood, should I marry and have children?"

Claudette replied, "Do you have someone in mind that you would like to marry?"

"No, but if I did I'd come back to asking you that same question. I cannot answer your question. It depends on the true openness of two people who love each other to make that decision."

The trip was pleasant, with stops in small towns and cities coming come to an end in New York City after six days of travel. They decided immediately to investigate passenger service to Amsterdam. A taxi driver took them to the Star Liner ticket office telling them that he had heard it was a good, clean, fast ship. They inquired at the ticket office for passenger service to Amsterdam. The clerk advised them that the Star Liner would dock in two days, re-supply on the third and sail for Amsterdam on the fourth day. The trip would take five days.

They decided to see the sights in and around the city finding it interesting how people seemed to ignore one another, always in a hurry to get somewhere. A boat ride out to the Statue of Liberty was a wonderful experience, along with the variety of food in so many restaurants. Claudette's call to the Star Liner ticket office informed that all passengers had to be aboard by eight in the morning with the ship leaving at eight-thirty. They told the desk clerk, to have them awakened at six, which would give them time to have breakfast and be aboard ship no later than seven-thirty.

Sleep was restless with the anxiety of returning to Paris taking up their thoughts. The phone rang at precisely six the next morning and they were eating their breakfast at six-thirty. They took a taxi to the ship dock where they presented their tickets of travel. Their luggage was marked and taken aboard the ship. Onboard the ship they were taken to their adjacent cabins, each with a view from their state room. They both walked out to the deck railing watching the tugboats pushing the liner into the open sea where once again they passed by the Statue of Liberty. The weather was warm and the seas were calm as the ship sliced through the water. A buffet was being served in the dining hall and they were told the formal dinner will be seated at seven in the evening. They immediately went to their rooms and had their best clothing sent out be washed and ironed and returned by six, which was gratifying considering what they look like.

Their clothing washed and ironed was returned to their state room at six. They were directed to the Captain's table and after many introductions of the people at that table, an abundance of food was placed on their plate. Alex looked at Claudette, who was surprised that no menu had been given to any of the people and were told that when sitting at the Captain's table you ate and drank the same food and drink that the captain was having. Dinner was good and the German wine had an excellent taste. Two hours later, after the captain and others had left the table, Claudette and Alex sat there drinking wine and discussing some of the food still on the table. They decided it was time to go to bed and wake up to enjoy the days ahead. Casually walking along the deck toward their state room, Claudette was reminiscing about her trip from New York City to Amsterdam and how she met Astin on that trip.

Standing by their state rooms Claudette said sleepily, "No tapping on my door until seven in the morning."

"I'll wake you at seven then, he said kissing her cheek

The following days were sunny with calm seas, making it a perfect time to rest and relax until they reached Amsterdam. They both were eager to get back into their own environment with Alex still having trouble trying to grasp the truth of his heritage; that he was of mixed blood and if he married there was always the possibility that the child could be black, causing damage to his family and friends. He was so deep in thought, that he hardly noticed the ship docking at pier. Only a call from Claudette, saying "Alex, come to your state room and finish packing. We will be getting off the ship in a very short time. Hurry, I do not want to linger! We need to get to the train station to buy our tickets for Paris. So hurry!"

Alex went to a state room and put his remaining pieces of this clothing in the small piece of luggage.

Claudette was at his door saying, "If you are ready, Alex, we can get to the gangplank before the crowd of people arrives." Leaving the ship, it was a short walk to the train station. She hurried ahead of Alex and purchased their tickets to Paris.

Alex looked at Claudette, and questioned, "Why are you in such a hurry to get home?"

She replied, "I am still so troubled over what Astin did that I need the security of our home. I cannot help myself because it keeps coming back in my mind. I hope it leaves when I get home, and start working again."

Alex responded by saying, "I wish we had not gone to America then I would have never known that I was of mixed blood. Now I have to cope with that knowledge for the rest of my life. What shall I do? Only time alone will give me the answers."

Back in Paris, Alex carried the small pieces of luggage to the bedrooms and soon heard the happy voices of the maid and cook.

"Would you like me to make a small dinner?"

"Yes that would be nice." Claudette replied.

In a very short time dinner was ready with soup and slices of white meat from a chicken that cook had prepared that morning. A glass of wine to excite the palate made for a very enjoyable meal. They both decided to go to bed early. The following morning they would go through the basket of mail that had accumulated in their absence.

The night passed swiftly, and when morning arrived, and Alex looked at his watch and it was already ten in the morning. He opened his bedroom door and yelled at to the cook, "I would like breakfast in a half hour, please."

Going into the kitchen he found Claudette was just finishing breakfast and leaving the table said, "I am going to sort the mail, and I will put those addressed to you in a small basket."

By the time Alex finishes breakfast and walks into the parlor Claudette had just finished separating all the mail.

Turning to Alex she said, "Most of our mail is dealing with our leather companies, lawyers and banking statements, you can read them when you are through with your personal mail."

The Letters

Alex opened up a letter from Pitor. Pitor wrote that there was much illness in his household with his wife and five year old child, dying from arsenic tainted waters from the well on his property. He does not know how much longer he will live because the medicine he is taking is very expensive and he was hopeful that I might be able to lend him some money so that he can continue his treatment for at least another year. "Please, Alex, help me. I need seven hundred dollars. Thank you, Pitor."

Alex saw the address on the back of the envelope that contained Pitor's letter and immediately called his bank and directed them to send the equivalent of two thousand dollars in Hungarian currency by special messenger to Pitor's home address with a return receipt signed by him that the money had been received. The bank responded by saying that his request would be done immediately, and that he will receive verification of the transaction in two days.

He opened a letter from Sylvia, which contained a photograph of her and three children. Reading the letter, Sylvia explained that the loving moments that they experienced together gave her the addition of twins to the family, "A boy that was white and a girl that was brown in color. My husband was extremely happy, thinking he was the proud father of twins. My three children, fathered by you, are a blessing in my life. My hope is that you will continue to keep our love affair and children a secret during our remaining years. You are the best and kindest person I have ever met. I will remember you always, Love Sylvia."

A letter from Lee Bisset was short and to the point, "Upon arrival from your trip in America would please call me at your earliest convenience to have dinner at the restaurant of your choosing. You have my telephone number. Lee B."

Alex went through the remainder of his mail which dealt with statements from the bank and the leather business. The following day he telephoned Lee, who was happy to hear his voice now that he had returned from America. They decided on dinner that evening at The Black Swan restaurant at six as a good place and time to meet. Alex told Claudette he was not going to have dinner at home and the reason was that he was going to have dinner with Lee Bisset.

Claudette teased Alex by saying, "Be careful, do not let Lee too close to you, she may take you into her clutches She laughed and said, "Do not take what I said seriously, Lee is a very bright woman who worked hard to get what she has now."

A Proposition

Alex arrived in the Black Swan restaurant promptly at six and found Lee had arrived before him and was seated at a table near the far end of the dining room. As Alex approached, he greeted Lee with a smile and a kiss on the cheek, saying, "What have you done to yourself? You look so vibrant and beautiful. What are you taking to look this way?"

Lee replied, "Sit down and I will show you."

Alex sat down with a curious look on his face then said, "All right, what are you going to show me?"

Lee rose from her chair and faced Alex who immediately saw that Lee was quite far along in her pregnancy. "You're going to have a baby?"

"Yes, WE are going to have a baby. I am happy for us, and I promise to accept all the help I can now and long after the child is born." Seeing his reaction, Lee snapped back, saying, "I suppose that what you said means that you are unsure of whether or not you are the father or someone else is the father? I was only in a one-time affair with a priest at the convent when I was seventeen. Since that time, I had never had sex or loved anyone until you entered my life. I did not plan to get pregnant, it just happened in a very loving relationship with you. I fell in love with you the first time we met and that feeling is still with me. You do not have to marry me and I will avoid seeing or meeting you."

Alex was overwhelmed by what Lee had just told him and said to her, "I need time to sort out what you had just told me. It must tell you in all honesty that I like you very much and I think my love will grow if we are together but I need time to sort all of our relationship."

The waitress, who had been coming to the table every forty-five minutes during that evening, told them the kitchen was closing in one hour, and she needed their order. Lee started to leave the table and told the waitress that she would not be ordering food.

Then, looking squarely into Alex's eyes, she angrily said, "I do not believe that he is ready for dinner either." She walked toward the exit not saying goodbye to Alex. Alex left a sizable tip for the waitress who said "I am sorry, sir, that you had a poor evening."

Alex, leaving the restaurant, was undecided as to whether he should go to Lee's house or return to his own place. He decided to go Lee's, as it was the right thing to do. Moments later he told the taxi driver to turn around and return to his house. Arriving at eleven-thirty, he was still very upset over the events of that evening and went directly to his bedroom. He fell asleep in a tired, depressed manner, tossing and turning with very little sleep, cursing himself over what had happened and what he had done.

Finally in the early morning, Claudette opened the bedroom door, asking Alex, "Are you awake?"

"Yes, I will have breakfast with you."

Alex dressed in his comfortable, casual attire and walked into the kitchen where Claudette was drinking a cup of coffee while the cook prepared breakfast.

Claudette looked at Alex and remarked, "You look very tired. It must have been an exhausting night. Do you think you can continue this kind of life? You are now forty-one years old. It is time to slow down Alex. If you do not, chances are that you will not live past fifty. Do not get upset with my teasing you. I want you to enjoy your life to the fullest."

Finishing breakfast, Alex turned to Claudette, asking her if she would sit down with him and have a serious talk.

Claudette, jokingly replied, "It is about marriage, is not it? Yes it is, I can see it in your eyes. Lee is a very intelligent woman, and you both make a beautiful couple."

"No mother, stop, you have it all wrong, very wrong. Now listen to what I have to say."

He then began to tell her. "He had a few affairs with Lee, one eight months ago, before we left for America. She claims that she loves me very much and was hopeful that I loved her also. I like her, but I do not love her. I just do not have a strong feeling about spending the rest of my life with her. Last night when we met for dinner, she told me that she was eight months into her pregnancy and feeling it was best to be married before the child was born. I was shocked over what she had told me, but I told her just what I am telling you, I am not ready for a long-term commitment and the pitfalls. I could not create a situation such as Astin did being born from mixed blood, which I will have the rest of my life."

There was a long moment of no words being spoken then Alex replied in a low whispering voice, "I do not want to be the father of a black child, one that is going to be hidden in an orphanage in the same way that Astin chose for his two sons."

Claudette replied by saying, "What if the baby is not black but white like you are? Would you be comfortable with marrying Lee?"

"No, that is not the point. The child will carry the stigma of mixed blood the rest its life."

Claudette suggested, "Maybe it would be best if you told Lee about your trip to America, where you found out that Astin was born into a mixed blood family."

Alex agreed that it was the proper thing to do. He telephoned Lee's house and when she answered, Alex replied, "There is something very important I have to tell you, can we meet somewhere?"

Lee replied, "Come to the house. I do not feel well enough to travel even a short distance."

Alex told Claudette he was going to see Lee, and he would call her before returning home. Arriving a short time later he found Lee, sitting in the parlor with reddened eyes and tears falling into a wet handkerchief.

Alex explained in the best way he knew what he had found out on his trip to America that his father Astin was born into a mixed blood family. That he was born white and his brothers and sisters were all dark skinned which meant that he was also a carrier of mixed blood. "Any child born of my conception would always carry a mixed blood gene with the possibility that the child could it be born white or black."

Hearing what Alex had said Lee shouted sarcastic and demeaning remarks with more foul language than he had ever heard before. She left the parlor and returned wearing her house robe. Alex looked at her and said, "Too many things are getting out of hand. It will be best if I call a cab and leave. We can discuss this, another day."

She stood there then walked slowly up to him and said, "Alex, I love you more than you will ever know. Goodbye, Alex. Goodbye my love."

She then reached in her house robe pocket and pulled out a small revolver, which she pressed against Alex's heart and pulled the trigger, firing two shots, while Alex looked in a complete surprise, saying his final words, "Why, Lee? Why!"

Lee looked at Alex lying there with his eyes fixed on the ceiling and closed each lid. Then she walked over to her favorite chair and fired one shot into her temple while saying goodbye to Alex in her final conscious mind.

The live-in housekeeper, Kate, who had living quarters in the lower level of the house, heard the gunshot's and rushed to the parlor where she saw Alex in a pool of blood on the floor. She looked toward Lee, who was slumped in her parlor chair with blood flowing from the right side of her forehead. She was breathing but coughing small amount of blood. Kate immediately called the police station and informed them about the shooting and the need for an ambulance to administer care to Lee. She was told to place and apply pressure with a face towel to the opening of Lee's head to stop the flow of blood which she did immediately. Precious time went by and finally the ambulance, followed by the police, arrived. They looked at Lee who was still breathing then asking Kate, if she knew how long Lee had been pregnant?

Kate replied, It has been 8 months."

The ambulance driver told the police that he was in his fourth year of learning to be a doctor and from what he could see if the baby was not removed by Cesarean method immediately then it would die along with its mother from lack of oxygen.

Lee was placed on the floor and the young man with a sharp knife opened up Lee's belly and brought out the child while his companion tied off the umbilical cord and gave the baby a soft slap on the back which brought a healthy cry from its mouth. Everyone was happy that the baby was alive. The umbilical cord was cut and the baby placed in some soft linen that Kate had brought into the room. Lee was in her last moments of life and finally her breathing stopped completely. The baby was taken to the hospital for special care. Alex and Lee were taken to the morgue for further investigation into their causes of death.

It was late evening and Alex had not called so Claudette surmised that they had solved their differences and Alex was going to spend the night with Lee. She decided to go to bed and would call him in the morning. At nine the following morning she received a telephone call from the police stating that her son was involved in a double suicide which looked after their investigation to be caused by Ms. Lee Bisset. "It appears Lee shot Alex and then took her own life by a bullet to her temple."

Claudette cried out, "Oh my God! Oh my God! How could this have happened?" fainted and fell to the floor. The cook and maid helped her into a chair and gave her some water to drink. The cook asked, "What is the matter? What caused you to faint?"

Claudette whispered, "I just received word from a policeman that Alex had been shot and is dead. There goes my life, the only joy that I had is now only emptiness and grief, Alex will always be my companion."

Two policemen came by in the late afternoon and questioned Claudette about any possible reason for this to happen?

"I think it was a lover's quarrel. They were trying to correct their problems."

The officer in charge then asked the question, "Did you know, that Lee Bisset was, according to her doctor, about to have a baby?"

"Yes. Alex mentioned it. Is the baby all right?"

"Yes, the baby was removed from Lee Bisset before she died and as of this morning when I called the hospital to inquire the condition of the baby, I was told that the baby was doing very well."

Claudette was stunned by the news she had received. Her eyes flooded with tears as the reality of what happened filled her mind. The officer gave her a card, which indicated where the bodies had been taken for further examination. He then expressed his condolences and left with his partner.

A rush of friends and employees from the leather company came to help her through this terrible time. The following days were like a stagnant blur in her mind and she would not accept what had happened until Alex was laid to rest next to Rea LeaBeau's grave. For the next week, Claudette sat in the parlor with a blank stare on her face somehow hoping that Alex would walk through the door and hug her as he always did. Then without thinking, she entered Alex's bedroom and decided to put some of his addressed letters to her in a folder. A letter from Astin slipped from a folder. Claudette took the letter to a nearby chair, sat down and began to read his writing.

"My Dear, Claudette:

I hope you will forgive me after you finish reading this letter. I have held the secret of my life from everyone in hopes of leading a pleasant and rewarding life but now I am ashamed for not allowing my secret to be known. My father married a slave, she gave birth to four colored brothers and sisters but I was born white into this mixed blood family. In my later years, I married a beautiful woman named Sally, who gave birth to one black son in Maryland and three years later, a black son in New Mexico. This drove her into drinking herself to death because she assumed that she was the cause of having black children. During our time in New Mexico, I had an affair with a young Indian girl, who months later had a black child. The white elders in town took the only young black man in town and hanged him for what he had supposedly done. That young Indian girl was killed along with her baby and burned to erase

*any bad omen on the tribe. I still kept my secret out of fear
and survival of my life. I resisted marrying you for that
reason and I do not know what I would have done if you
had a black child. I thank God that he was born white, to
enjoy a happy life.*

My deepest love to you,

Astin"

Sitting there and thinking about what she had just read. She
decided to stop living in the past and enjoy her time in the present
and future. She took a taxi to the hospital where the baby was being
kept. In the maternity ward she asked the nurse to see the baby of
Lee Bisset. The nurse went to a small crib at the far end of the room
and brought the baby close to Claudette.

The nurse said, "He is a fine looking boy. Don't you think? Look,
he has a small amount of blond hair, and his skin is as white as snow.
Are you, his grandmother?"

"Yes, I am and hope to be for a very long time."

She handed the baby to Claudette, who began to cry as she held
him gently in her arms. "When will I be able to take him home?"

The nurse replied, I will get an answer from the doctor and let
you know, by phone."

On her way out Claudette stopped at the reception desk and
asked for the name of the ambulance driver and if he was on duty
at the present time?

The receptionist pointed to a door with a red cross and said, "He
would be in that room. His name is Luis Omere."

Claudette entered the room and seeing only one man reading
from a very heavy book said, "Are you Luis Omere?"

"Yes, I am. Can I help you?"

Claudette replied "I have been told that you are the person that
did a Cesarean operation on Lee Bisset to save the unborn child
moments before she died."

"Yes I did and I am happy that he had no complications and
should grow up to be a fine young man."

Claudette questioned Luis about his studying to become a doctor. Luis stated that he had at least four more years which were in studies and internship at the hospital.

"But," he added, "With the time spent working as a medical assistant on the ambulance, I doubt very much that I can complete everything in that time as I have to continue working to save enough money to pay for my college tuition."

Claudette withdrew her checkbook from her pocket, and without asking Luis wrote him a check for a hundred thousand dollars.

Luis looked at the amount and said to Claudette. "This must be a mistake!"

"No," Claudette replied. "That is a small amount for saving the life of my grandson. Here is my card and if you ever have the need for financial assistance, you can call me at this number."

Secrets are a shield that continues to fester until they are seen by others as a contagious weakness to be avoided. Stop and look in a mirror to see a true reflection of who you are, not on the surface, but inside your mind and heart. There are many of us who carry our silent secrets to the end of our lives, never intending to divulge their existence to anyone.

The End